# William Shakespeare's 2 Henry IV, aka Henry IV, Part 2: A Retelling in Prose

David Bruce

Published by David Bruce, 2022.

This is a work of fiction. Similarities to real people, places, or events are entirely coincidental.

WILLIAM SHAKESPEARE'S 2 HENRY IV, AKA HENRY IV, PART 2: A RETELLING IN PROSE

**First edition. July 21, 2022.**

Copyright © 2022 David Bruce.

ISBN: 979-8201301415

Written by David Bruce.

# Table of Contents

# Dedication

**Dedicated to Carl Eugene Bruce and Josephine Saturday Bruce**

My father, Carl Eugene Bruce, died on 24 October 2013. He used to work for Ohio Power, and at one time, his job was to shut off the electricity of people who had not paid their bills. He sometimes would find a home with an impoverished mother and some children. Instead of shutting off their electricity, he would tell the mother that she needed to pay her bill or soon her electricity would be shut off. He would write on a form that no one was home when he stopped by because if no one was home he did not have to shut off their electricity.

The best good deed that anyone ever did for my father occurred after a storm that knocked down many power lines. He and other linemen worked long hours and got wet and cold. Their feet were freezing because water got into their boots and soaked their socks. Fortunately, a kind woman gave my father and the other linemen dry socks to wear.

My mother, Josephine Saturday Bruce, died on 14 June 2003. She used to work at a store that sold clothing. One day, an impoverished mother with a baby clothed in rags walked into the store and started shoplifting in an interesting way: The mother took the rags off her baby and dressed the infant in new clothing. My mother knew that this mother could not afford to buy the clothing, but she helped the mother dress her baby and then she watched as the mother walked out of the store without paying.

***

The doing of good deeds is important. As a free person, you can choose to live your life as a good person or as a bad person. To be a good person, do good deeds. To be a bad person, do bad deeds. If you do good deeds, you will become good. If you do bad deeds, you will become bad. To become the person you want to be, act as if you already are that kind of person. Each of us chooses what kind of person we will become. To become a good person, do the things a good person does. To become a bad person, do the things a bad person does. The opportunity to take action to become the kind of person you want to be is yours.

Human beings have free will. According to the Babylonian Niddah 16b, whenever a baby is to be conceived, the Lailah (angel in charge of contraception) takes the drop of semen that will result in the conception and asks God, "Sovereign of the Universe, what is going to be the fate of this drop? Will it develop into a robust or into a weak person? An intelligent or a stupid person? A wealthy or a poor person?" The Lailah asks all these questions, but it does not ask, "Will it develop into a righteous or a wicked person?" The answer to that question lies in the decisions to be freely made by the human being that is the result of the conception.

A Buddhist monk visiting a class wrote this on the chalkboard: "EVERYONE WANTS TO SAVE THE WORLD, BUT NO ONE WANTS TO HELP MOM DO THE DISHES." The students laughed, but the monk then said, "Statistically, it's highly unlikely that any of you will ever have the opportunity to run into a burning orphanage and rescue an infant. But, in the smallest gesture of kindness — a warm smile, holding the door for the person behind you, shoveling the driveway of the elderly person next door — you have committed an act of immeasurable profundity, because to each of us, our life is our universe."

In her book titled *I Have Chosen to Stay and Fight*, comedian Margaret Cho writes, "I believe that we get complimentary snack-size portions of the afterlife, and we all receive them in a different way." For Ms. Cho, many of her snack-size portions of the afterlife come in hip hop music. Other people get different snack-size portions of the afterlife, and we all must be on the lookout for them when they come our way. And perhaps doing good deeds and experiencing good deeds are snack-size portions of the afterlife.

The Zen master Gisan was taking a bath. The water was too hot, so he asked a student to add some cold water to the bath. The student brought a bucket of cold water, added some cold water to the bath, and then threw the rest of the water on a rocky path. Gisan scolded the student: "Everything can be used. Why did you waste the rest of the water by pouring it on the path? There are some plants nearby which could have used the water. What right do you have to waste even a drop of water?" The student became enlightened and changed his name to Tekisui, which means "Drop of Water."

# Educate Yourself
# Read Like A Wolf Eats
# Be Excellent to Each Other
# Books Then, Books Now, Books Forever

***

In this retelling, as in all my retellings, I have tried to make the work of literature accessible to modern readers who may lack some of the knowledge about mythology, religion, and history that the literary work's contemporary audience had.

Do you know a language other than English? If you do, I give you permission to translate this book, copyright your translation, publish or self-publish it, and keep all the royalties for yourself. (Do give me credit, of course, for the original retelling.)

I would like to see my retellings of classic literature used in schools, so I give permission to the country of Finland (and all other countries) to give copies of this book to all students forever. I also give permission to the state of Texas (and all other states) to give copies of this book to all students forever. I also give permission to all teachers to give copies of this book to all students forever.

Teachers need not actually teach my retellings. Teachers are welcome to give students copies of my eBooks as background material. For example, if they are teaching Homer's *Iliad* and *Odyssey*, teachers are welcome to give students copies of my *Virgil's* Aeneid: *A Retelling in Prose* and tell students, "Here's another ancient epic you may want to read in your spare time."

# CAST OF CHARACTERS

**Male Characters**

Rumor, the Presenter

*King, and Supporters of the King*

King Henry IV

Henry, son of Henry IV; Prince of Wales; afterwards King Henry V; also known as Prince Hal and as the younger Harry

Prince Thomas of Clarence, son of Henry IV

Prince John of Lancaster, son of Henry IV

Prince Humphrey of Gloucester, son of Henry IV

Earl of Warwick

Earl of Westmoreland

Earl of Surrey

Gower

Harcourt

Sir John Blunt

Lord Chief Justice of the King's Bench

A Servant of the Lord Chief Justice

*The Rebels*

Earl of Northumberland

Richard Scroop, the Archbishop of York

Lord Mowbray

Lord Hastings

Lord Bardolph

Sir John Colevile

Travers and Morton, retainers of the Earl of Northumberland

*Male Eastcheap Characters*

Sir John Falstaff

His Page, a boy

Bardolph

Pistol

Ned Poins

Peto

*Other Male Characters*

Robert Shallow, and Silence, country justices

Davy, Servant to Robert Shallow

Ralph Moldy, Simon Shadow, Thomas Wart, Francis Feeble, and Peter Bullcalf, recruits

Fang and Snare, sheriff's officers

**Female Characters**

Lady Northumberland

Lady Percy, widow of Hotspur, a rebel

Mistress Quickly, hostess of Boar's Head Inn, a tavern in Eastcheap

Doll Tearsheet, prostitute

**Other Characters**

Lords and Attendants; Porter, Drawers, Beadles, Servants, Strewers of Rushes, etc.

A Dancer, speaker of the epilogue

**Scene**: England

**Note**: Shakespeare frequently collapses time in his history plays. For example, in *2 Henry IV*, the incident at Gaultree Forest, the Battle of Bramham Moor, and the death of King Henry IV all occur very close in time.

In history, the incident in which the Archbishop of York was tricked occurred in 1405. He died on 8 June 1405.

In history, the Battle of Bramham Moor, in which Northumberland was defeated, occurred on 19 February 1408.

In history, the death of King Henry IV occurred on 20 March 1413.

In 5.2 appears a reference to "Amurath." This information comes from *Oxford Reference* and *The Oxford Dictionary of Phrase and Fable* (2 ed.): "The name of several Turkish sultans. Amurath in 1574 murdered his brothers on succeeding to the throne, and his successor in 1596 did the same. Shakespeare alludes to this in *Henry IV, Part 2* (1597), when the dying king admonishes his son, 'This is the English, not the Turkish court; Not Amurath an Amurath succeeds, but Harry, Harry.'"

Actually, the character who says, "This is the English, not the Turkish court; Not Amurath an Amurath succeeds, but Harry, Harry" (5.2.47-49 in the Signet Classic edition) is the new king: Henry V, formerly Prince Hal.

https://www.oxfordreference.com/display/10.1093/oi/
authority.20110803095409923

https://www.oxfordreference.com/display/10.1093/acref/
9780198609810.001.0001/acref-9780198609810

(Both accessed 3 March 2024.)

# INDUCTION

At Warkworth, in front of the castle of the Earl of Northumberland, the figure of Rumor, dressed in a cloak on which were painted many tongues, appeared.

Rumor said, "Open your ears; for who of you will block the vent of hearing when loud Rumor speaks? I, from the Eastern orient to the West where the Sun droops and sets, making the wind my horse to spread rumors widely and quickly from post to post, continually unfold and disclose and spread 'news' of the actions commenced on this ball called Earth. Slanders continually ride upon my tongues. In every language I pronounce these slanders, stuffing the ears of men with false reports. I speak of peace, while hidden hatred that disguises itself as smiling safety wounds the world.

"And who but Rumor — who but only I — causes gatherings of soldiers and preparations for defense because of fear when the pregnant year is thought to be with child by the stern tyrant war, although that is not true, and the year is swollen because of some other grief.

"Rumor is a pipe — a wind instrument — blown by surmises, jealousies, and conjectures. This pipe has well-defined holes with which to produce the musical notes, and it can be so easily played that the blunt monster with uncounted heads — the always discordant and wavering multitude of people — can play upon it.

"But why should I anatomize my well-known body to you? You know this already.

"So why is Rumor here? I run before King Henry IV's victory. In a bloody field by Shrewsbury, the King and his army have beaten down the young rebel Hotspur and his troops, quenching the flame of bold rebellion with the rebels' blood.

"But why am I telling you the truth right now, here at the beginning? My job is to spread misinformation. My job is to noise abroad the 'news' that Harry Monmouth — Prince Hal, heir to the throne — fell under the wrath of noble Hotspur's sword, although in truth Prince Hal killed Hotspur at the Battle of Shrewsbury on 21 July 1403. My job is to noise abroad the 'news' that King Henry IV fell before the rage of the Scottish nobleman Archibald, Earl of

"

Douglas. I am spreading the false news that the King's anointed head stooped as low as death before the Douglas.

"These falsehoods I have rumored through the peasant towns that lie between that royal field of Shrewsbury and this worm-eaten hold of ragged stone at Warkworth, where Hotspur's father, the aged Earl of Northumberland, lies crafty-sick — he feigns illness as an excuse for not bringing an army to the Battle of Shrewsbury, preferring to let others do the hard and dangerous work of fighting.

"Exhausted, the messengers come riding hard to bring him news, and not a man of them brings news other than what they have learned from me. From Rumor's tongues — my tongues — they bring untrue good news. This false news raises hopes that will be dashed. Hearing false news of good things is worse than hearing true news of bad things — it is better to know the worst immediately than to have your hopes raised and then dashed."

# CHAPTER 1

## — 1.1 —

At Warkworth, in front of the castle of the Earl of Northumberland, Lord Bardolph, a rebel, approached the gate and called, "Who guards the gate here?"

The porter opened the gate, and Lord Bardolph asked, "Where is the Earl of Northumberland?"

The porter asked him, "Who shall I say you are?"

"Tell the Earl of Northumberland that the Lord Bardolph wishes to speak to him."

"His lordship is walking in the garden. If it pleases your honor, go and knock at the garden gate, and he himself will answer the knock."

The Earl of Northumberland walked toward the porter and Lord Bardolph, who saw him and said, "Here comes the Earl."

The porter departed and Northumberland asked, "What is the news, Lord Bardolph? Every minute now should be the father of some violent deed. The times are wild, and contention, like a horse that is full of over-rich feed, madly has broken loose and tramples everyone in its path."

"Noble Earl, I bring you true and certain news from Shrewsbury."

"Good news, I hope, if God wills it!"

"It is news as good as your heart can wish," Lord Bardolph said. "King Henry IV is wounded and near death. As for Hotspur, your son, he has slain Prince Hal. The Douglas has killed both Blunts: Sir Walter Blunt and Sir John Blunt."

This was another of Rumor's lies. Sir Walter Blunt had been killed, yes, but Sir John Blunt still lived.

Lord Bardolph continued, "Young Prince John and Westmoreland and Stafford fled from the battlefield."

This was another of Rumor's lies. Stafford died on the battlefield, and Prince John and Westmoreland were victorious and did not flee.

Lord Bardolph continued, "Hotspur took prisoner Prince Hal's brawny friend, the fattened boar known as Sir John Falstaff. He is as big as the hulk of a large merchant ship.

"Oh, such a day and such a battle, so fought, so followed, and so fairly won, has not so dignified the times since the days of Julius Caesar!"

"How do you know this?" the Earl of Northumberland asked. "Did you see the battlefield? Have you come from Shrewsbury?"

"I spoke with one, my lord, who came from Shrewsbury. He is a gentleman who is well bred and of good name, and he freely told me this news and said that it is true."

Northumberland looked up and said, "Here comes my servant Travers, whom I sent last Tuesday to listen for news."

"My lord, I rode past him on the way here," Lord Bardolph said. "He can have no news other than the news that I have brought to you."

Northumberland said, "Now, Travers, what good tidings come with you?"

Travers said, "My lord, I met Sir John Umfrevile, who talked to me and gave me joyful tidings. I therefore turned back to return here. Sir John Umfrevile had a better horse than I had, and so he rode quicker than I. After Sir John had outdistanced me, another horseman came spurring hard. He was a gentleman, almost exhausted because of his speedy riding, and he stopped by me to let his bloodied horse rest. He asked me for directions to Chester; and I demanded to know what news he was bringing from Shrewsbury. He told me that the rebellion had bad luck and that young Harry Percy's spur was cold. With that, he gave his able horse the head, and bending forward he struck his spurs against the panting sides of his poor nag up to the rowel-head, and they seemed in running to devour the road, and he stayed no longer to answer questions."

Northumberland said, "Tell me again: Did he say that young Harry Percy's spur was cold? Is Hotspur now Coldspur? Did he say that the rebellion had met ill luck?"

Surprised by the news, Lord Bardolph said, "My lord, I'll tell you this: If my young lord, Hotspur, your son, has not won the battle, then I swear upon my honor that I will trade all my land for a silken lace that is used to tie clothing such as stockings. Do not talk about defeat."

Northumberland asked, "Why then did that gentleman who rode by Travers speak about defeat?"

"Who, he?" Lord Bardolph said. "He was some worthless and base fellow who had stolen the horse he was riding, and, I swear upon my life, he spoke without a foundation of fact."

Lord Bardolph looked up and saw Morton coming toward them. He said, "Look, here comes more news."

Northumberland looked at Morton and said, "This man's brow is like a title page that reveals much information about the tragedy written inside the book."

Title pages occasionally reveal much information. For example, this is written on the title page of the 1597 edition of *Richard III*: "The Tragedy of King Richard the third. Containing, His treacherous Plots against his brother Clarence: the pittiefull murther of his innocent nephewes: his tyrannicall usurpation: with the whole course of his detested life, and most deserved death."

Northumberland said, "By looking at Morton's brow, I can see that he has bad news. His brow looks like the shore on which a powerful flood has left signs of its devastation. His brow is furrowed."

He then said, "Say, Morton, did you come from Shrewsbury?"

Morton replied, "I ran from Shrewsbury, my noble lord. At Shrewsbury, hateful death put on his ugliest mask to frighten our party of rebels."

"How are my son and my brother?" Northumberland asked, "You tremble, and the whiteness in your cheek is more able than your tongue to tell your errand. A man like you, as faint, as spiritless, as dull, as dead in look, as woebegone, drew back the bed-curtain of Priam, King of Troy, and would have told him that half of his sacked city was burning, but Priam saw the fire before the man could move his tongue. I know that Hotspur, my son, is dead even before you can speak to me. I know that you would tell me, 'Your son did thus and thus; your brother did thus and thus; the noble Douglas fought and did thus and thus.' You would fill my greedy ears with their bold deeds, but in the end, you would sigh and say something that will blow away all this praise: 'Your brother, your son, and all are dead.'"

Morton said, "Douglas is living, and your brother is still alive so far, but as for your son, Hotspur —"

"Why, he is dead," Northumberland said. "See what a ready tongue suspicion has! A man who fears something and does not wish it to be true, can by instinct learn from seeing another's eyes that what he feared would happen has in fact happened. Yet speak, Morton. I am an Earl, and I outrank you, but tell me that I am wrong. I will take my being wrong as a sweet disgrace and make you a rich person for doing me such wrong."

"You are too great to be lied to by me," Morton said. "Your instinct is too correct, your fears too certain."

Northumberland said, "Yet, for all this, do say not that Hotspur, my son, is dead."

He looked at Morton and added, "I see a strange confession in your eye. You shake your head, and you are afraid to speak the truth or you think that it is a sin to speak the truth. If Hotspur has been slain, say so. The tongue that truthfully reports his death does not offend. The person who sins is the person who tells me that my son is still alive when he is really dead. The person who tells me that a dead person is dead and not alive does not sin. Yet it is true that the first bringer of unwelcome news has a thankless task. Ever afterward, his voice will sound like a sullen and sad funeral bell; his voice will be remembered for tolling the death of a friend."

"I cannot think, my lord, that your son is dead," Lord Bardolph said.

"I am sorry that I should force you to believe that which I wish to God I had not seen," Morton said, "but these eyes of mine saw him in a bloody state, only faintly fighting back, wearied and out of breath, as he faced Prince Hal, whose swift wrath beat down the never-daunted Percy to the earth, from whence he never again sprung up alive. Briefly, the death of Hotspur, whose spirit lent a fire even to the dullest peasant in his camp, becoming known, immediately took fire and heat away from the best-tempered courage in his troops. By Hotspur's metal and mettle, the rebels were steeled. Once Hotspur died and his mettle abated and his metal weakened, all the remaining rebels turned back and fled, like a weak sword made of dull and heavy lead that bends and turns back onto itself. A heavy thing such as a heavy-duty arrow can swiftly fly when force is applied to it. Our rebel warriors were heavy with sadness at Hotspur's death, and this heaviness combined with their fear lent so much lightness to their feet that arrows fled not swifter toward their aim than did our soldiers, aiming at their safety, fly from the field.

"During the retreat, the noble Worcester — your brother — was too soon taken prisoner; and that furious Scot, the bloody Douglas, whose well-laboring sword had three times slain noblemen who dressed like Henry IV to serve as decoys, began to lose his courage and did grace the shame of those who turned their backs by joining them in flight, and in his flight, stumbling in fear, he was captured.

"The summary of all is that King Henry IV has won the Battle of Shrewsbury, and he has sent out a fast-moving army to encounter you, my lord. This army is under the command of both young Prince John of Lancaster and the Earl of Westmoreland. This is very important news."

"For this I shall have time enough to mourn," Northumberland said. "In poison there is physic, aka medicine; and this news, which if I had been well would have made me sick, has instead made me, a sick person, to some degree well. A wretch can have fever-weakened joints that are like useless hinges and buckle under him, but when he has a fit, he breaks like a fire out of his keeper's arms. Just like that, my limbs, weakened with grief, have now enraged with grief, and are three times stronger than they were before."

He threw his cane to the side and said, "Go hence, therefore, you effeminate crutch! A gauntlet with joints of steel and overlapping metal pieces must now be the glove for this hand."

He threw his nightcap to the side and said, "Go hence, you sickly invalid's cap! You are a guard too effeminate for my head — a head that Princes, having turned living soldiers into corpses during their victory in the Battle of Shrewsbury, aim to hit. Now bind my brows with an iron helmet, and let approach the roughest hour that time and spite dare to bring to frown upon the enraged Northumberland!"

He then called for the subversion of order: "Let the Heavens crash and kiss the Earth! Now let not Nature's hand keep the wild flood confined — let the waters flood the land! Let order die! And let this world no longer be a stage to feed contention and battle in a lingering, long-lasting act. Instead, let the spirit of Abel-killing Cain, the first murderer, reign in all bosoms. That way, each heart will set itself on bloody and murderous courses, and the rude and violent scene will end, and darkness will bury the dead!"

Lord Bardolph said, "This too-strong emotion does you ill, my lord."

"Sweet Earl, divorce not wisdom from your honor," Morton said to Northumberland. "Do not overreact with extreme emotion. The lives of all your faithful accomplices rest on your health. If you give yourself over to stormy passion, your health must and will decay.

"You thought about the outcome of the war, my noble lord, and you thought about the chances of victory before you said, 'Let us gather an army.' You knew that it was a possibility that, in the exchange of blows, your son might drop and die. You knew that he walked over perils as if he were walking on the edge of a cliff and that he was more likely to fall off than to reach safety. You knew that his flesh was capable of receiving wounds and scars and that his courageous spirit would take him where the most danger ranged. Yet you told him, 'Go forth.' None of this, although you definitely understood it to be a possibility, could restrain the deliberately carried out battle. What then has happened? What has this bold enterprise brought forth? Only what you knew was likely to happen."

Lord Bardolph said, "All of us who suffered this loss knew that we ventured on such dangerous seas that it was ten to one against us that we would stay alive, and yet we ventured to rebel against King Henry IV because our possible gain outweighed our likely defeat. We have suffered a defeat, but let us venture again. Come, we will all put forth, body and goods. Let us continue our rebellion. We will risk our lives and our possessions."

"This is the appropriate time for rebellion," Morton said. "My most noble lord, I hear for certain, and I do speak the truth, that the well-born and noble Archbishop of York is rebelling and has raised well-equipped armies. He is a man who with a double surety binds his followers: He has both temporal and spiritual authority, and so his soldiers will follow him both bodily and spiritually. Hotspur, your son, had only the bodies — the shadows and mere appearances — of his men fighting for him. The word 'rebellion' affected his soldiers. It separated the action of their bodies from their souls, and they fought only with queasiness, not all out; they were like men who were drinking medicine. Their weapons seemed to be on our side, but the word 'rebellion' froze their spirits and souls like fish freezing in an icy pond. But now the Archbishop of York makes insurrection a religion; rebellion has become a holy act. He has the reputation of being sincere and holy in his thoughts, and so he is followed both with the body and with the mind. He gathers support for the rebellion by using the blood of fair King Richard II, who was murdered at the castle in Pomfret — the King's blood was scraped from Pomfret stones. The Archbishop of York has made Heavenly his quarrel and his cause. He tells his followers that this land is bleeding and gasping for life under King Henry IV, and both high-born and low-born flock to follow him."

"I knew of this before," Northumberland said, "but, to say the truth, my present grief had wiped it from my mind. Go in with me; and let every man come up with ideas on how best to get safety and revenge. We will get messengers to carry our letters, and we will make new allies quickly. Never have we had so few soldiers, and never have we had more need for soldiers."

On a street in London, Sir John Falstaff and his page, a boy who acted as his servant, stood and talked. Falstaff's page was carrying his sword and small, round shield. Prince Hal had assigned the page to serve Falstaff.

Falstaff said to the boy who was his page, "You giant, what says the doctor about my urine?"

Falstaff had given a urine sample to a doctor.

The page replied, "He said, sir, the urine itself was a good healthy urine, but that the person who gave the urine sample might have more diseases than he could tell."

"Men of all sorts take pride in mocking me," Falstaff said. "The brain of this foolish compound of clay, man, is not able to invent anything that tends to laughter, more than I invent or more than is invented on me. I am not only witty in myself, but I am also the cause of the wit that is in other men. I do here walk before you like a sow that has crushed all her litter but you, her remaining piglet. If the Prince put you into my service for any other reason than to annoy me, why then I have no intelligence. You whoreson mandrake, you are fitter to be worn in my cap than to wait at my heels. You are no bigger than a brooch — an agate stone set in silver or gold — that can be worn as a decoration on a cap. I was never served by an agate stone until now, but I will inset you neither in gold nor silver; instead, I will place you in vile clothing, and send you back again to your master, Prince Hal, as a jewel — I will give you back to the juvenal — the juvenile — who is the Prince your master, whose chin is not yet covered with down. I will sooner have a beard grow in the palm of my hand than he shall get one on his cheeks, and yet he will not hesitate to say that his face is a face-royal. God may finish his face when He will by letting Prince Hal grow a beard. So far, Prince Hal's face does not have a single hair amiss. Prince Hal may keep his face-royal because the face of his royal father, King Henry IV, appears on the face of the coin known as a royal, and Prince Hal need not spend that coin by getting a shave from a barber — no barber shall ever earn sixpence out of Prince Hal's royal. And yet Prince Hal crows and boasts as if he had been a full-grown man ever since his father was a bachelor and Prince Hal was not yet born. He may keep his own royal grace, but he's almost out of my grace, I can assure him. Yes, he can keep his title of Prince of Wales, but he is almost out of my favor, I can assure him."

Falstaff hesitated and then asked his page, "What did Master Dombledon say about the satin for my short cloak and my wide breeches?"

"He said, sir, you should procure him better assurance of being paid than Bardolph can provide," the page replied. "He would not take his word and he said that he would not take yours; he wants better assurance of being paid."

Falstaff greatly wanted to wear extravagant clothing; he much less wanted to pay for it.

"Let him be damned, like the glutton!" Falstaff said. "I pray to God that his tongue grow hotter!"

Falstaff was referring to the parable of the rich man and the pauper in Luke 16:19-31. The pauper died and went to Heaven; the rich man died and went to Hell. The rich man wanted the pauper to dip his finger in water so that he could shake some drops onto the rich man's tongue, but Abraham, who was in Heaven, pointed out that this is not permitted.

Falstaff continued, "He is a whoreson Achitophel!"

Now Falstaff was referring to Achitophel, a counselor to King David. When Absalom rebelled against David, Achitophel supported Absalom. This story is told in 2 Samuel 15. Say what you will about Falstaff, he knew much about the content of the Bible.

Falstaff continued, "He is a rascally yea-forsooth good-for-nothing! He hints that an answer of 'yes' is forthcoming when he does not mean it. He encourages a gentleman to hope for credit, and then he asks for security. These whoreson shopkeepers wear short hair and high shoes and have bunches of keys at their girdles; and if a man has made an honest agreement with them, then they insist upon a guarantee of payment. I would just as soon they would put rat poison in my mouth as put guarantee of payment in it. I expected that he would send me twenty-two yards of satin, as I am a true knight, and instead he sends me notice that I must guarantee that I will pay him so that payment is secure. Well, he may sleep in security because he has the horn of abundance. He has the horn of plenty, and he has the horns of a cuckold, and the heels of his wife are light when she raises them in the air when she sleeps with other men, and he does not see that although he has his own lanthorn — a lantern whose light shines through thin sheets of horn — to provide light for him."

He paused and then asked, "Where's Bardolph?"

This Bardolph was an alcoholic crony and most definitely was not the rebel Lord Bardolph.

The page replied, "He's gone into Smithfield to buy your worship a horse."

Falstaff said, "I hired Bardolph in St. Paul's, and he'll buy me a horse in Smithfield. If I could get myself a wife from the brothels, I would be manned, horsed, and wived."

Unemployed men used to hang around St. Paul's Cathedral, hoping to find work. Horses that were bought in Smithfield had the reputation of being nags. Most men would not think that a prostitute would make a good wife. A then-current proverb stated, "Who goes to Westminster for a wife, to Paul's for a man, or to Smithfield for a horse, may meet with a whore, a good-for-nothing, and a jade." Many brothels were in Westminster.

The Lord Chief Justice and his servant walked toward Falstaff and his page. Falstaff was not a fan of officials who enforced the law. Earlier, Prince Hal had gotten angry at the Lord Chief Justice, who was punishing one of Prince Hal's friends for committing a crime. Prince Hal struck the Lord Chief Justice, who, acting under the authority of Prince Hal's father, King Henry IV, threw him in jail.

The page said, "Sir, here comes the nobleman who committed Prince Hal to jail when the Prince struck him during an argument."

"Wait nearby," Falstaff said. "I will pretend that I do not see him."

The Lord Chief Justice saw Falstaff, thought that he recognized him, and asked his servant, "Who is that man walking away from us?"

"He is Falstaff, if it please your lordship."

"That man who was more than a suspect in the robbery on Gad's Hill?"

"Yes, my lord," the servant replied, "but he has since done good service at the Battle of Shrewsbury, and I hear that he is now going with some charge of soldiers to fight in the army of Prince John of Lancaster."

"What? He is going to fight the Archbishop of York?" the Lord Chief Justice said. "Call him to come over to me."

"Sir John Falstaff!" the servant called.

Falstaff said to his page, "Boy, tell him I am deaf."

The page said, "You must speak louder; my master is deaf."

The Lord Chief Justice said, "I am sure he is, when it comes to the hearing of anything involving justice."

He said to his servant, "Go and pluck him by the elbow; I must speak with him."

The servant obeyed his orders and said loudly, "Sir John!"

Falstaff said to the Lord Chief Justice's servant, whom he pretended was a slacker and a beggar, "What! A young good-for-nothing, and begging! Are there not wars? Is there not employment? Doesn't the King lack subjects to fight for him? Don't the rebels need soldiers? Though it is a shame to be on any side but one — the side of King Henry IV — it is worse shame to beg than to be on the worst side — the side of the rebels, assuming that anything can be worse than rebellion."

The servant said, "You are mistaken about me, sir."

Falstaff said, "Why, sir, did I say you were an honest man? Setting aside my knighthood and my soldiership, both of which make it likely that I am telling the truth, I would have lied in my throat if I had said that you are an honest man."

"Please, sir, then set aside your knighthood and your soldiership," the servant said, "and give me leave to tell you that you lie in your throat, if you say that I am anything other than an honest man."

"Me give you leave to tell me that!" Falstaff said. "Me set aside that which belongs to me! If I give you leave, then hang me. If you take leave, then hang yourself! When you hunt, you go in the wrong direction — away from your prey — and now you are confronting the wrong man. Leave! Go away!"

The servant said, "Sir, my lord wants to speak with you."

The Lord Chief Justice said, "Sir John Falstaff, I want to have a word with you."

"My good lord!" Falstaff said. "May God give your lordship a good day. I am glad to see that your lordship is out and about. I had heard that your lordship was sick, and so I hope your lordship goes abroad by the advice of a doctor. Your lordship, though you are not clean past your youth, you have yet some taste of age in you, some relish of the maturity of time; and I must humbly beg your lordship to take care of your health."

"Sir John, I sent for you so I could talk to you officially before your expedition to Shrewsbury," the Lord Chief Justice said.

"If it please your lordship," Falstaff said. "I hear his majesty has returned with some discomfort and ill health from Wales."

"I am not talking about his majesty," the Lord Chief Justice said. "You would not come when I sent for you."

Falstaff continued, "And I hear, moreover, his highness has fallen into this same whoreson paralysis."

Falstaff was subtly threatening the Lord Chief Justice. One day King Henry IV would die, and Prince Hal would become King Henry V. Falstaff thought that things would then go badly for the Lord Chief Justice. After all, the Lord Chief Justice had once thrown Prince Hal in jail, and Falstaff would have the ear of King Henry V.

The Lord Chief Justice declined to be intimidated, saying, "Well, may God heal King Henry IV! Please, let me speak with you."

"This paralysis is, as I take it, a kind of lethargy, if it please your lordship; it is a kind of sleeping in the blood, a whoreson tingling."

"Why are you telling me about it?" the Lord Chief Justice asked. "Let it be as it is."

"This paralysis has its origin from much grief, from study and perturbation of the brain," Falstaff said. "I have read the cause of its effects in the medical treatise written by the ancient Greek physician Galen. It is a kind of deafness."

"I think that you have the same disease," the Lord Chief Justice said, "because you are not hearing anything that I say to you."

"Very well, my lord, very well," Falstaff said. "In fact, if it please you, I have the disease of not listening, the malady of not paying attention. That is the malady that troubles me."

"I can very easily cure your disease of not paying attention when I speak to you," the Lord Chief Justice said. "All I have to do is put your feet in a pair of stocks and immobilize you and expose you to the scorn of passersby. I would rather enjoy being your physician."

"I am as poor as Job, my lord, but not as patient as Job," Falstaff replied. "Your lordship may minister the potion of imprisonment to me because I am poor and so cannot pay a fine, but that I should be your patient and follow your prescriptions, some wise men may take some slight exception — they may have part of a scruple about it or even a whole scruple."

Falstaff thought, *I have a high friend — Prince Hal — who visits low places, such as taverns in Eastcheap. The Lord Chief Justice, if he is wise, should remember that.*

The Lord Chief Justice said, "I sent for you, when there were matters against you that could cost you your life, to come speak with me. You were accused — and definitely identified by eyewitnesses — of being involved in the robbery on Gad's Hill, and that is a capital offense."

"As I was then advised by my learned counsel in the laws of my military service, I did not come," Falstaff said. "Because I was doing military service, I was immune from your civilian summons."

"Well, the truth is, Sir John, you have a bad reputation," the Lord Chief Justice said. "You live in great infamy."

Falstaff, who had an enormous beer — or wine — belly, said, "Anyone who buckles himself in my belt cannot live in less than greatness."

"Your financial means are very slender, and your waste is great," the Lord Chief Justice said.

Falstaff replied, "I wish it were otherwise; I wish my financial means were greater, and my waist slenderer."

"You have misled the youthful Prince."

"The young Prince has misled me," Falstaff said. "I am the fellow with the great belly, and he is my dog that walks in front of me."

"Well, I am loath to pick at a newly healed wound: Your day's service at the Battle of Shrewsbury has a little gilded over your night's exploit on Gad's Hill," the Lord Chief Justice said. "You may thank this unquiet time of rebellion against the King for your quietly not being punished for that robbery."

"My lord?" Falstaff said.

"But since all is well, keep it so," the Lord Chief Justice said. "Wake not a sleeping wolf."

"To wake a wolf is as bad as to smell a fox," Falstaff said.

"To smell a fox" was proverbial for "To be suspicious."

The Lord Chief Justice was unhappy at hearing this remark. He was not suspicious that Falstaff had committed a robbery; he was certain that Falstaff had committed a robbery.

"What! You are like a candle, more than half of which has burned," the Lord Chief Justice said. "Anyone can smell the smoke rising from you."

"I might be a wassail candle, my lord, made of all tallow," Falstaff said. "A wassail candle is a large candle that is meant to burn all night, and you can see that I am large. Wassail candles are also made of tallow, aka animal fat, and you can see that I am largely made of animal fat. If I were to say, however, that I were made of wax, my growth would make some people think that I was telling the truth: My waist waxes; it does not wane."

"There is not a white hair on your face but should have its effect of gravity," the Lord Chief Justice said. "A white beard denotes old age, which should denote seriousness."

"Each white hair on my face denotes gravy, gravy, gravy," Falstaff said.

"You follow the young Prince Hal up and down, like his evil angel."

"That is not true, my lord," Falstaff replied. "Lucifer was an angel of light, but anyone who looks at me can see that I am not light. Angels are coins that can be trimmed by cutting off the edges and so removing some of the precious metal. The only way to see whether they are good angels is to weigh them; if they are light angels, then they are bad angels. Anyone who looks at me need not weigh me to determine that I am not light.

"Yet, in some respects, I grant, I cannot go and I cannot tell. I cannot pass current: I am out of step with modern times. Virtue is of so little regard in these petty-shopkeeper times that a man of true valor takes a lowly job as a keeper of tame bears, a man of true wit takes a job as a tapster and wastes his quickness of intellect by not speaking except to tell customers how much they owe, and all the other gifts that are pertinent to man are not worth a gooseberry, according to the malice of this age that determines what is to be regarded as valuable.

"You who are old do not value the capacities of us who are young; you measure the heat of our lives with the bitterness of your lives, and we who are in the front lines of our youth, I must confess, are wags, too. We who are young have spirit."

The Lord Chief Justice was surprised to hear Falstaff speak as if he were a young man — Falstaff was obviously old.

The Lord Chief Justice said, "Do you set down your name in the scroll of youth? Your name, Falstaff, has been written down in the scroll of the old — you have all the characteristics of old age. Have you not a moist eye? A dry hand? A yellow cheek? A white beard? An unsteady leg? An increasing belly? Is not your voice broken? Is not your wind short? Is not your chin double? Is not your wit single? Is not every part of you blasted with antiquity and old age? And will you yet call yourself young? For pity, Sir John!"

The Lord Chief Justice was a good man who made very few mistakes, but he did make a mistake here. Falstaff's chin was double, but his wit was not single. Falstaff was a master of the pun, in which a word has a double meaning — or more. Falstaff's wit was most definitely double.

Falstaff replied, "My lord, I was born about three of the clock in the afternoon, with a white-haired head and something of a round belly."

Falstaff was telling the truth. He was a fictional character created by William Shakespeare, and the play he was performing in often was performed in the afternoon.

He continued, "As for my voice, I have lost it with hallooing and the singing of anthems. I will not give more evidence of my youth. The truth is that I am only old in judgment and understanding; I have the wisdom of old age. But if anyone wants to compete against me in a dancing contest for a thousand marks — a lot of money — then let him lend me the money, and let us compete!

"As for the box on the ear that Prince Hal gave you, he gave it like a rude Prince, and you took it like a sensible lord. I have rebuked him for it, and the young lion repents. True, he does not repent in ashes and sackcloth; instead, he repents in new silk and with old wine."

"Well, may God send the Prince a better companion!" the Lord Chief Justice said.

"May God send the companion a better Prince!" Falstaff said. "I cannot get rid of Prince Hal."

"Well, King Henry IV has separated you and Prince Harry," the Lord Chief Justice said. "I hear that you are going with Prince John of Lancaster to fight against the Archbishop of York and the Earl of Northumberland. King Henry IV and Prince Hal are going elsewhere."

"Yes, I thank your pretty sweet wit for it," Falstaff said. He thought that the Lord Chief Justice had persuaded the King to keep Prince Hal and Falstaff separate.

He added, "But all of you who stay at home and kiss my Lady Peace, please remember to pray that the opposing armies do not join in battle on a hot day because, by the Lord, I am taking only two shirts with me, and I hope not to sweat extraordinarily. If the battle occurs on a hot day, and I brandish anything but a bottle, I hope that I will never spit white again. Spitting red is the result of suffering from tuberculosis or being wounded in battle.

"There is not a dangerous action that peeps out his head but I am thrust upon it. If a battle needs to be fought, I have to go to the battle. Well, I cannot last forever, but it has always been the custom of our English nation that if they have a good thing, they make it too common by using it continually. If you must say that I am an old man, you should give me rest. I wish to God that my name were not as terrible and frightening to the enemy as it is. I would prefer to be rusted to death than to be worn down to nothing through perpetual work."

The Lord Chief Justice replied, "Well, be honest, be honest; and God bless your expedition!"

Falstaff, who was accustomed to borrow but not to repay money, asked, "Will your lordship lend me a thousand pounds to equip myself for the expedition?"

"Not a penny, not a penny," the Lord Chief Justice said. "You are too impatient to bear crosses: You are too quick to borrow coins stamped with a cross. Fare you well, and commend me to my kinsman Westmoreland."

The Lord Chief Justice and his servant exited.

"If I do, hit me with a three-man beetle," Falstaff said.

A three-man beetle is a hammer or battering ram so big and heavy that it takes three men to use it to drive stakes or to flatten paving stones.

He added, "A man can no more separate old age and covetousness than he can part young limbs and lechery. The gout galls the old, and the pox — venereal disease — pinches the young. Both stages of life anticipate my curses. I am greedy for money. In addition, I am suffering either from the gout or from the pox — venereal disease."

Falstaff then called, "Boy!"

"Sir?"

"How much money is in my wallet?"

The page replied, "Seven groats and two pence. A groat is worth four-pence, and so you have thirty pence."

Because he was Falstaff's page, the boy carried Falstaff's wallet and money.

Falstaff complained, "I can get no remedy against this consumption of my wallet. Borrowing increases the amount of time that I have money to spend, but quickly the contents of my wallet are again consumed. This kind of consumption is an incurable disease.

"Go, and take this letter to my Prince John of Lancaster; take this letter to Prince Hal, and take this letter to the Earl of Westmoreland."

Because everyone falsely believed that Falstaff had killed Hotspur during the Battle of Shrewsbury, he had a military reputation that he did not deserve, and he was a figure of some importance. Prince Hal had killed Hotspur, but he allowed Falstaff to take the credit.

Falstaff added, "Take this letter to old Mistress Ursula, whom I have weekly sworn to marry ever since I perceived the first white hair on my chin.

"Go now. You know where to find me when you have finished your errands."

The page left to deliver the letters.

Falstaff said to himself, "A pox on this gout! Or, a gout on this pox! The one or the other plays the rogue with my big toe and makes it painful. But it does not matter if I limp. I march under the colors of a battle flag, and those colors can cover the real reason for my limp — I will pretend that I was injured in the war, and that will make my being paid a pension seem more reasonable. A good intelligence can make good use of anything; I will turn my diseases into profit."

The Archbishop of York and the lords Hastings, Mowbray, and Bardolph were meeting at the Archbishop's palace.

"Now you know the reasons for our rebellions and you know the resources we have," the Archbishop of York said. "Please, my most noble friends, speak plainly your opinions of our hopes. Is this rebellion likely to succeed? Lord Mowbray, you speak first. What is your opinion?"

"I agree that we have adequate reasons to rebel," Lord Mowbray said, "but given the resources we have, I would like to be better satisfied that we can be strong enough to confidently face the power and puissance of King Henry IV."

Lord Hastings said, "According to our records, our present muster consists of twenty-five thousand picked troops. Our hope of reinforcements lies largely in the great Earl of Northumberland, whose bosom burns with an incensed fire of injuries. He is angry because his son and his brother died at Shrewsbury."

Lord Bardolph said, "The question then, Lord Hastings, is this: Will our twenty-five thousand troops be enough to defeat Henry IV's troops without reinforcements from Northumberland?"

"If we receive reinforcements from Northumberland, we can defeat King Henry IV," Lord Hastings said.

"Yes, we can, by Mother Mary," Lord Bardolph said, "but we need to ask whether we will be too weak to defeat the King without Northumberland's help. In my opinion, we ought not to fight the King until we are sure that Northumberland will fight with us. In a matter as bloody-faced and as serious as this, we ought not to rely on conjecture, expectation, surmise, and false hopes. We must be sure that we will have reinforcements."

"You speak very truly," the Archbishop of York said. "We remember what happened to Hotspur at Shrewsbury. He expected reinforcements from his father, Northumberland, but those reinforcements never came."

"My lord, Hotspur fed himself with false hope," Lord Bardolph said. "He ate the air, which contained nothing more than promises of reinforcements. He flattered himself that an army was coming to help him, but that army was much smaller than the smallest of his thoughts: It was nonexistent. And so, with the great imagination that is proper to madmen, he led his troops to their death and he closed his eyes as he leapt to his destruction."

Lord Hastings said, "But, by your leave, it does not hurt to think about the likelihood of good things happening."

Lord Hastings was an optimist; Lord Bardolph was a realist.

"Yes, it does hurt," Lord Bardolph said. He was a practical man. At the Battle of Shrewsbury, Northumberland had not arrived with reinforcements; would he arrive at a future battle? Lord Bardolph wanted to know what he could count on for sure, and what he could count on for sure was 25,000 troops — 25,000 troops that might never be augmented.

"If this war we are engaged in, this battle we are planning, this fight against the King, is based only on hope, then it does hurt us — it can get us killed the way that it got Hotspur killed," Lord Bardolph said. "If we base our plans and actions on hope, then we are like a farmer who sees buds on his orchard trees in early spring. Should the farmer simply hope that the buds will become ripe fruit, or should he be aware of the likelihood that frosts will kill the buds and destroy the potential fruit? In such a case, despair is more appropriate than hope.

"When we mean to build a house, we first survey the plot, and then we draw up the plan of the house. When we see the plan of the house, then we must estimate the cost of its construction. If we find that the house will cost more to build than we can afford to pay, what do we then but draw up a new plan for the house, one with fewer rooms — or we decide not to build the house.

"What we are planning now is much bigger and more important than a house. The great work in front of us is to tear one Kingdom down and then set up a new Kingdom. Given the importance of this work, we must carefully consider the situation and the plan, we must make sure that we have a firm foundation, we must question surveyors and architects and get expert opinions, we must know our resources and how likely we are to succeed in undertaking this work, and we must consider opposing evidence and arguments that we shall not succeed.

"If we do not do this, then we invest our lives in paper and in written figures, and we invest our lives in the names of men instead of in men. We allow our lives to depend on reinforcements that exist only in hope and not in reality.

We will be like a man who draws the plan of a house that is beyond his ability to build it. We will be like a man who, halfway through building the house, is forced to give up and leave his partly created and costly house exposed to the weeping and rainy clouds; his house is turned by the tyranny of churlish winter into waste."

"Let us suppose that we have no hope of receiving reinforcements from Northumberland, although in my opinion we do have good hopes of receiving the reinforcements," Lord Hastings said. "Let us suppose that our army is now at its largest and strongest. I think we have an army strong enough, right now, to fight the King on equal terms."

"What, does the King's army consist of only twenty-five thousand troops?" Lord Bardolph asked.

Lord Hastings replied, "No more troops than that will oppose us, Lord Bardolph. In fact, not even that many troops will oppose us. The King's soldiers, in these violent times, have been divided into three armies. One army opposes the French. One army opposes Glendower and his Welsh soldiers. That leaves the third army to oppose us. The King is unfirm and weak, and his soldiers are divided into three armies. In addition, his treasury echoes with the sound of hollow poverty and emptiness."

The Archbishop of York said, "We need not dread that King Henry IV will gather his three armies together and come against with us with full force."

Lord Hastings said, "If he were to do that, he would leave his back unarmed, and the French and Welsh soldiers would be biting his heels. We need never fear that the King will come against us with all his troops."

"Who is likely to lead his forces against us?" Lord Bardolph asked.

"Prince John of Lancaster and the Earl of Westmoreland," Lord Hastings said. "King Henry IV and his son, Prince Hal, will fight Glendower and his Welsh troops. I am not sure who will lead the King's troops against the French."

The Archbishop of York said, "Let us continue our rebellion and fight the King's soldiers." Although he was not a military man, he was making the decision to fight the King's soldiers.

He continued, "We will publicly proclaim the reasons for our rebellion. The citizens of the commonwealth are sick of their own choice; they chose Henry IV instead of Richard II. Their over-greedy love has stuffed them, and they are sick of King Henry IV.

"Whoever builds on the hearts of the common people has a house that is giddy, foolish, and unsure; it is as if he built his house on sand rather than granite. Oh, you foolish many, with what loud applause did you beat the sky with your blessings of Bolingbroke, before he became what you would have him be: Henry IV! And now you have him, and you, beastly feeders, are so full of him that you provoke yourselves to vomit him up. You common dogs disgorged your glutton bosom of the royal Richard II, and now you want to eat your dead vomit up, and you howl as you try to find it. What trust can be found in these times? Those who, when Richard II lived, wanted him to die, are now enamored of him although he is now in his grave. You, who threw dust upon Richard II's goodly head when through proud London he came sighing as he followed the admired heels of Bolingbroke, you now cry, 'Oh, earth, give us King Richard II again, and you take King Henry IV!' Oh, thoughts of accursed men! To you, the past and the future seem best; the present seems worst."

Lord Mowbray asked, "Shall we assemble our soldiers and march?"

Lord Hastings said, "We are time's subjects, and time bids us be gone. It is time to march."

# CHAPTER 2

## — 2.1 —

On a street in London, Mistress Quickly met Fang, a police sergeant. Following behind him was his assistant, Snare.

"Master Fang, have you filed my lawsuit?" Mistress Quickly asked. She often gave people titles higher than the ones they actually had. Such was the case with "Master" Fang now.

"I have filed it," Fang said.

"Where's your yeoman — your assistant?" Mistress Quickly asked. "Is he a lusty, strong yeoman? Will he stand up for me?"

Anyone who knew Mistress Quickly knew that she was often unintentionally bawdy. "Stand up for me" could be interpreted as referring to a male body part that could at times be erect. That male body part could be referred to as a weapon.

Fang looked to each side and did not see his assistant. He said to himself, "Where's Snare?"

Mistress Quickly called, "Master Snare!"

Snare walked up behind them and said, "Here I am; here I am."

"Snare, we must arrest Sir John Falstaff," Fang said.

"Yes, good Master Snare," Mistress Quickly said. "I have filed a lawsuit against him."

"It may perhaps cost some of us our lives," Snare said, "because he will stab."

"Then it will be a bad day!" Mistress Quickly said. "Be careful around Falstaff; he stabbed me in my own house, and that most beastly. Truly, Falstaff does not care what mischief he does. If his weapon is out, he will thrust it like any Devil; he will spare neither man, woman, nor child."

A person with a bawdy sense of humor could laugh at the thought of Falstaff stabbing Mistress Quickly with his "weapon."

"If I can get close enough to him to grab him," Fang said, "I won't care about his thrust."

"No, and I won't either," Mistress Quickly said. "I'll be at your elbow."

"If I can hit him once," Fang said, "if he comes within my grasp —"

"I am undone by his going to fight in the war," Mistress Quickly said. "He will leave without paying me what he owes me. I promise you, he owes me an infinitive amount of money on his tab."

By "infinitive," Mistress Quickly meant "infinite."

She continued, "Good Master Fang, be sure to restrain him. Good Master Snare, let him not escape. He comes continuantly to Pie Corner — saving your manhoods — to buy a saddle."

By "continuately," Mistress Quickly meant a combination of "continuously" and "incontinently." By "saving your manhoods," she was apologizing for bringing up an unsavory topic. "Pie Corner" was known for its squealing pigs and its smell of food cooking. It also had shops that sold cattle, and other places where women rented their "pies." Falstaff was going to war, but he already had a saddle, and he had no need to go to Pie Corner "continuously" and "incontinently" to buy saddles, except that men such as Falstaff rode prostitutes and "saddle" was slang for female genitals and for a prostitute.

She continued, "Falstaff is indited to dinner with Master Smooth's the silkman at the Lubber's Head on Lumbert Street."

By "indited," she meant "invited." By "the Lubber's Head," she meant "The Leopard's Head." A "lubber" is a big and clumsy fellow.

She continued, "Please, since my exion is entered [action, aka lawsuit, has been filed] and my case so openly known to the world, let Falstaff be brought in to answer."

Again, Mistress Quickly was unintentionally bawdy. A woman's "case" is a good place in which to sheath a penis, and she had said that her case is "so openly known to the world." By the way, the Latin word *vagina* means "sheath."

She added, "A hundred marks is a long one for a poor lone woman to bear." Falstaff's tab had a hundred marks on it and it was a long tab and he owed Mistress Quickly a hundred marks — marks are units of money.

She continued, "I have borne, and borne, and borne, and have been fubbed off, and fubbed off, and fubbed off, from this day to that day, that it is a shame to be thought on. Falstaff will not pay me the money he owes me. There is no honesty in such dealing; unless a woman should be made an ass and a beast, to bear every good-for-nothing's wrong."

She looked up, saw Falstaff, and said, "Yonder he comes; and that errant malmsey-nose good-for-nothing, Bardolph, with him. Malmsey is a red wine, and Bardolph has a red nose from drinking so much wine. Do your offices, do your offices, Master Fang and Master Snare. Do me, do me, do me a favor and do your offices."

An eavesdropper might have laughed after hearing Mistress Quickly urge Fang and Snare to "do me, do me."

Falstaff and Bardolph walked over to Mistress Quickly, Fang, and Snare. Falstaff's page was with him.

"How are you?" Falstaff asked. They were looking at him oddly, so he asked, "Whose mare's dead?" This was a way of asking, "What's the fuss?"

He added, "What's the matter?"

Fang said, "Sir John, I arrest you at the suit of Mistress Quickly."

Falstaff resisted arrest: "Go away, varlets! Draw your sword, Bardolph, and cut off this villain's head for me, then throw the harlot in the gutter."

"Throw me in the gutter!" Mistress Quickly said. "I'll throw you in the gutter. Would you do that? Would you? You bastardly rogue!"

"Bastardly" was Mistress Quickly's combination of "Bastard" and "Dastardly." "Dastardly" means "cowardly."

She cried, "Murder, murder! Ah, you honeysuckle villain! Will you kill God's officers and the King's? Ah, you honey-seed rogue! You are a honey-seed, a man-queller, and a woman-queller."

Mistress Quickly had mixed up her words again. By "honeysuckle" and "honey-seed," she meant "homicidal" — she was accusing Falstaff of being a man-killer and a woman-killer.

"Keep them away from me, Bardolph," Falstaff ordered.

Fang shouted, "A rescue! A rescue!"

Often, when a man was being arrested for debt, his friends would come and rescue him and help him flee from the officers of the law.

Mistress Quickly, who thought that Fang was calling for reinforcements, asked the people around her, "Good people, bring a rescue or two."

She said to Falstaff, "You will, will you? You will, will you? Do, you rogue! Do, you hemp-seed!"

Hangmen's ropes were made of hemp, and Mistress Quickly was saying that Falstaff would someday become intimately acquainted with a hangman's noose.

Falstaff shouted, "Go away, you scullion — you lowly kitchen servant! Go away, you rampallion — you ramping strumpet! Go away, you fustilarian —

you fustilug, aka fat, frowsy woman! I'll tickle your catastrophe — I'll whip your posterior!"

The Lord Chief Justice and some of his men arrived on the scene.

"What is the matter?" the Lord Chief Justice said. "Keep the peace here!"

"My good lord, be good to me," Mistress Quickly said. "I beg you to stand up for me."

The Lord Chief Justice recognized Falstaff and said, "How are you, Sir John? Why are you brawling here? Does this become your place, your time, and your business? You should have been well on your way to York by now."

He said to Fang, "Stand back and away from him, fellow. What are you charging him with?"

Mistress Quickly said, "Oh, most worshipful lord, if it please your grace, I am a poor widow of Eastcheap, and Falstaff is being arrested at my suit."

As she often did when talking to people, she addressed him by a better title than he had earned. Royalty, Dukes, and Archbishops are called "grace."

The Lord Chief Justice could guess that the dispute was over money that Falstaff had borrowed but not paid back. He asked, "For what sum?"

"It is more than for some, my lord; it is for all — all I have," Mistress Quickly replied. "He has eaten me out of house and home; he has put all my substance into that fat belly of his."

She said to Falstaff, "But I will have some of it out again, or I will ride you of nights like the mare."

Falstaff knew that she meant "nightmare," but he punned, "I think I am as likely to ride the mare, if I have any vantage of ground to get up."

Being able to get a leg up is an advantage when it comes to riding a mare — or a woman. And when someone weighs as much as Falstaff, it helps to stand on higher ground while climbing onto a saddle.

"How comes this to be, Sir John?" the Lord Chief Justice said. "For pity! What man of good temper would be able to endure this tempest of exclamation? Are you not ashamed to force a poor widow to undertake such a drastic action as a lawsuit in order to get what is owed to her?"

Falstaff asked Mistress Quickly, "What is the gross sum that I owe you?"

Mistress Quickly replied, "By Mother Mary, if you were an honest man, you would know that you owe me yourself and the money, too. You swore to me upon a partly gilded goblet, while you were sitting in the Dolphin room of my inn, at the round table, by a coal fire, on Wednesday of Whitson week, when Prince Hal broke your head for comparing his father to a singing-man of Windsor who was an imposter and a pretender to the throne, you swore to me then, as I was washing your wound, to marry me and make me my lady your wife. Can you deny it? Did not goodwife Keech, the butcher's wife, come in then and call me gossip Quickly? She came in to borrow some vinegar, and she told us that she had some good prawns. You wanted to eat some, but I told you that they were bad for a fresh wound. And did you not, when she was gone downstairs, tell me to be no more so familiarity with such poor people; saying that before long they should call me madam?"

Words about social classes are important when social classes are important. If Mistress Quickly were to marry Sir John Falstaff, a knight, she would be called "lady" and "madam" instead of such familiar terms as "goodwife" and "gossip," aka friend and neighbor. By the way, although Mistress Quickly may have frequently misused words, she had a large multi-syllable vocabulary. By "familiarity," she meant "familiar."

She continued, "And did you not kiss me and ask me to bring you thirty shillings? I put you now to your book-oath: Put your hand on the Bible, and deny that what I had said is true, if you can."

Falstaff said to the Lord Chief Justice, "My lord, this is a poor mad soul; and she says up and down the town that her eldest son looks just like you. She has been wealthy, but the truth is that poverty has made her insane. As for these two foolish officers, I beg you that I may have redress against them — they have committed a wrong against me by attempting to arrest me."

"Sir John, Sir John, I am well acquainted with your manner of wrenching the true cause the false way," the Lord Chief Justice said. "You want to make it appear that you have been wronged when, in fact, you have wronged this woman. It is not a confident brow — your false appearance of innocence — nor the throng of words that come with very much more than impudent sauciness from you, that can keep me from forming an unbiased judgment. You have, as it appears to me, manipulated the easily manipulated spirit of this woman, and made her serve your uses both in purse and in person."

"Yes, that is true, my lord," Mistress Quickly said.

"Please, be quiet," the Lord Chief Justice said to her.

He then said to Falstaff, "Pay her the debt you owe her, and unpay the villany you have done her. Make things right. You can pay her the debt you owe her with money, and you can unpay the villany you have done her with sincere apology and repentance."

"My lord, I will not undergo this sneap — this snub — without reply," Falstaff replied. "You mistake honorable boldness for impudent sauciness. You believe that a man who bows before you and says nothing is a virtuous man, but no, my lord, with all due respect, I will not bow down before you. I say to you that I desire deliverance from these officers. They ought not to arrest me because I must quickly attend to the business that King Henry IV wants me to do."

"You speak as if you have the power to do wrong — to commit a crime and get away with it," the Lord Chief Justice said. "You have a certain status and reputation. Live up to your status and reputation, and make things right with this woman. No one should be above the law."

"Come here, hostess," Falstaff said to Mistress Quickly. They talked together quietly.

Gower, who was carrying a message, walked up to the Lord Chief Justice, who said, "Now, Master Gower, what is the news you have for me?"

Gower replied, "The King, my lord, and Harry the Prince of Wales are nearby. This message tells the rest of the news."

Falstaff said to Mistress Quickly, "I swear as a gentleman. Come. Agree to lend me some money. Let us talk no more about this."

"By this Heavenly ground I tread on, I will have to pawn both my plate and the tapestries in my dining rooms," Mistress Quickly said. She had combined two well-known expressions, "By this Heavenly light" and "By this ground I tread on."

"Glasses, glasses is the only material to use for drinking," Falstaff said. "Glass is replacing plate — metal such as pewter. As for your walls, you can replace your tapestry with a comic painting, or a depiction of the parable of the Prodigal Son, or a German boar-hunting scene painted on imitation tapestry. One of those is worth a thousand of these cheap bed-curtains and these fly-bitten tapestries. Let me borrow ten pounds, if you can. Come, if it were not for your moods, there would not be a better wench than you in all of England. Go, wash your face, and withdraw your lawsuit. Come, you must not be mad at me. Don't you know me better than that? Come, come, I know that someone persuaded you to do this."

"Please, Sir John, let the loan be only twenty nobles."

A noble was a gold coin worth about a third of a pound.

She continued, "Truly, I am loath to pawn my plate, so help me."

Falstaff said, "Forget about it. I will find somebody else. You will always be a fool."

"Well, you shall have the money," Mistress Quickly said, "even if I have I pawn my gown. I hope you'll come to supper. You'll pay me back all you owe me?"

"Will I live?" Falstaff said.

He whispered to Bardolph, "Go with her. Follow her closely, and make sure that she does not change her mind."

"Will you have Doll Tearsheet meet you at supper?" Mistress Quickly asked.

"Yes, but let's have no more talking," Falstaff said. "Invite her to dinner."

Mistress Quickly, Bardolph, Fang and Snare, and the page left.

The Lord Chief Justice said to Gower about the King's campaign in Wales, "I have heard better news."

Falstaff asked, "What's the news, my lord?"

Ignoring Falstaff, the Lord Chief Justice asked Gower, "Where did the King sleep last night?"

Gower replied, "At Basingstoke, fifty or so miles from London, my lord."

"I hope, my lord, all's well," Falstaff said. "What is the news, my lord?"

Continuing to ignore Falstaff, the Lord Chief Justice asked, "Did all the King's forces come back?"

"No," Gower replied, "fifteen hundred foot soldiers and five hundred soldiers on horseback are marching to join Prince John of Lancaster and fight against Northumberland and the Archbishop of York."

The Archbishop of York and other leaders of the rebellion had not anticipated that soldiers who had been delegated to fight the Welsh would be reassigned to fight the rebels in the North of England.

"Is the King coming back from Wales, my noble lord?" Falstaff asked.

Continuing to ignore Falstaff, the Lord Chief Justice said to Gower, "You shall receive letters to deliver from me quickly. Come, let's go, good Master Gower."

Falstaff shouted, "My lord!"

The Lord Chief Justice asked, "What's the matter?"

Ignoring the Lord Chief Justice, Falstaff said, "Master Gower, will you have dinner with me?"

"I must serve my good lord here," Gower replied, "but I thank you, good Sir John."

"Sir John, you loiter here too long," the Lord Chief Justice said. "You are supposed to be busy recruiting soldiers as you travel to join Prince John of Lancaster and the Earl of Westmoreland."

Ignoring the Lord Chief Justice, Falstaff said, "Will you dine with me, Master Gower?"

"What foolish master taught you these manners, Sir John?" the Lord Chief Justice asked.

Ignoring the Lord Chief Justice, Falstaff said, "Master Gower, if my manners do not become me, he was a fool who taught them to me."

He meant that he had learned his manners — ignoring someone who spoke to him — from the Lord Chief Justice.

He said to the Lord Chief Justice, "This is the right fencing style, my lord — tap for tap, and tit for tat — and so we are even."

"Now may the Lord lighten you — enlighten you and make you lighter!" the Lord Chief Justice said. "You are a great big fool."

Prince Hal and one of his Eastcheap friends, Ned Poins, talked together on a street in London.

Prince Hal, who had just traveled from Wales, said, "By God, I am exceedingly weary."

"Are you really?" Poins asked. "I would have thought weariness would not have dared to take into custody one who is born as highly as you."

"Truly, weariness has attached itself to me," Prince Hal said. "I admit it although it discolors the complexion of my greatness to acknowledge it. I now have the pallor of weariness. Does it not reflect badly on me to want to drink small — thin and weak — beer right now?"

"Why, a Prince should not be so loosely studied as to remember so weak a composition," Poins said.

Poins was capable of wit. He was punning on "loosely studied," which means both "badly educated" and "versed in immoral — that is, loose — matters." In addition, he was punning on "weak composition," which means both "a badly written work" and "watered down and low in alcoholic content."

"It is likely then that my appetite was not Princely got," Prince Hal said, "for, truly, I do now remember and desire to drink the poor creation that we call small beer. But, indeed, these humble considerations distance me from my greatness. I am a Prince and a future King, but I do not act like it, and I do not have the tastes of a nobleman.

"What a disgrace is it to me to remember your name! Or to remember and know your face tomorrow! The high and mighty do not recognize the faces of the common people. What a disgrace is it to me to know how many pairs of silk stockings you own! You have one pair that you are wearing now, and you have a pair that were peach-colored! What a disgrace is it to me to know the inventory of your shirts! You have the shirt you are wearing now, and you have one more shirt. But the proprietor of the tennis courts knows how many shirts you have better than I because when you lack shirts you do not play tennis because sweating requires one or more changes of shirts. You have not played tennis for a long time because your low countries — your nether regions — have eaten up your Holland — your shirts that were made of cloth manufactured in

Holland. You pawned one or more shirts in order to go to one or more bawdy houses. You may have lost possession of your shirts, but the world has gained in population — you have fathered bastards. God knows whether those infants who bawl out from the ruins of your linen shall inherit His Kingdom, but the midwives say the children are not at fault for being bastards. They are not responsible for the sins of their parents. Because of fornication in bawdy houses, the population of the world increases, and families are mightily strengthened with the addition of members."

"How ill it follows, after you have labored so hard in Wales, that you should talk so idly!" Poins said. "Tell me, how many good young Princes would do so when their fathers are as sick as yours is at this time?"

"Shall I tell you something, Poins?" Prince Hal asked.

"Yes, you may — and let it be an excellent good thing."

"It shall serve among wits of no higher breeding than your own."

"Go on and tell me," Poins said. "I can stand whatever your something is that you will tell me. I can take whatever you say to me, so speak frankly to me and I will speak frankly to you."

"By Mother Mary, I will tell you," Prince Hal said. "It is not fitting that I should be sad, now that my father is sick. However, let me tell you, because you are a person whom, for want of a better man, I call my friend, that I could be sad because of my father's illness — very sad, indeed."

"That does not seem likely," Poins said. He was thinking that when Henry IV died, Prince Hal would become Henry V, and who would not want to be King?

"I swear by my hand that you think that I am as far in the Devil's book as you and Falstaff are for obduracy and stubbornness and persistency: Let the end try the man. But I tell you that my heart bleeds inwardly because my father is so sick. Unfortunately, my keeping such vile company as you has necessarily taken from me all show of sorrow."

"What is the reason that you cannot show sorrow for your father's illness?" Poins asked.

"What would you think of me, if I should weep?"

Poins spoke frankly: "I would think you are a most Princely hypocrite."

"Everyone would think the same thing," Prince Hal said, "and you are blessed to think as every man thinks: No one's thoughts have ever cleaved more to popular opinion than your thoughts. Every man would think that I am a hypocrite indeed. And what induces your most worshipful thought to think that?"

"Why, because you have been so loose-living and so closely attached to Falstaff."

"And to you," Prince Hal said.

Poins replied, "I swear by God's light that people speak well of me; I can hear it with my own ears. The worst that they can say of me is that I am a second brother and that I am a proper fellow with my hands. Because I am a second brother, I will not inherit my father's estate, and being good with my hands, I can fight well. Those two things, I confess, I cannot help. At times, I need to fight."

He looked up and said, "By the Mass, here comes Bardolph."

Bardolph, accompanied by Falstaff's page, walked over to Prince Hal and Poins. The page was dressed in an odd-looking uniform that Falstaff had given to him.

Prince Hal said, "Coming with Bardolph is the boy whom I sent to Falstaff to be his page. When I sent the boy to Falstaff, he was dressed like a Christian. Look at the boy now: Falstaff has dressed him in the costume of a performing monkey."

Bardolph said, "May God save your grace!"

Prince Hal replied, "And may God save you, most noble Bardolph!"

Poins, making fun of Bardolph's face, which was red because of his alcoholism, said to him, "Come, you virtuous ass, you bashful fool, must you be blushing? Why are you blushing now? What a maidenly soldier have you become! Is it such a blushing matter to take the maidenhood of — to drink up and empty — a pottle-pot that holds two quarts of beer or wine?"

The page also made fun of Bardolph's face: "Just now, my lord, he called to me from the other side of the red lattice of a window at the inn, and I could not tell what was his face and what was the window. At last I spied his eyes, and I thought that he had made and peeped through two holes in the badly reputed ale-wife's new red petticoat."

Prostitutes were known for wearing red petticoats.

"Has not the boy profited from being around Falstaff?" Prince Hal said sarcastically to Poins.

Bardolph, who was sensitive about his face, said to the page, "Go away, you whoreson upright rabbit, go away!"

The page replied, "Go away, you rascally Althaea's dream, go away!"

"Instruct us, boy," Prince Hal said. "Teach us. What dream are you referring to, boy?"

"My lord, Althaea dreamed that she gave birth to a fire-brand. Bardolph's face is red like a firebrand, and therefore I call him her dream."

Prince Hal knew that Falstaff's page was mixing up two dreams. Althaea was the mother of the ancient Greek hero Meleager. Shortly after he was born, she dreamed that he would live as long as a piece of wood on the fire remained unburned. She woke up, removed the piece of wood from the fire and kept it safe. But after the adult Meleager killed her brothers, Althaea placed the piece of wood on a fire. It burned up, and Meleager died. The second dream was that of Hecuba, wife of King Priam of Troy. She dreamed that she gave birth to a firebrand. The son she gave birth to was Paris, who ran away with Helen, the wife of King Menelaus of Sparta, and fled with her back to Troy. Helen became Helen of Troy, and Menelaus and a Greek army fought a war with the Trojans to get her back.

Prince Hal said to the boy, "That is a crown's worth of good interpretation. Here, take this crown — this coin — boy."

Poins could also be generous, despite his poverty. He said, "I hope that this good blossom — this page — can be kept from cankers — from things that would hurt him! Well, here is sixpence to preserve you."

Bardolph said, "If this boy does not end up being hanged someday, the gallows shall have been wronged and deprived of its rightful prey."

"Bardolph, how is your master, Falstaff?"

"He is well, my lord," Bardolph replied. "He heard of your grace's coming to town. His page has a letter for you."

The page handed a letter to Prince Hal, and Poins said, "You have delivered the letter with the proper ceremony."

Poins then asked Bardolph, "And how is the Martlemas, your master?"

In calling Bardolph's master "Martlemas," Poins referred to the fattened pigs and cattle that were slaughtered on November 11 — the feast of St. Martin — to be provisions for the winter. In other words, he was calling Falstaff a fat cow or a fat pig.

Bardolph, who understood to whom Poins was referring, replied, "His body is healthy, sir."

Poins said, "By Mother Mary, it is his immortal part that needs a physician, but Falstaff does not care. Although his soul is sick, it will not die."

Prince Hal, who had glanced at Falstaff's letter to him, said, "I allow this wen — this wart, this lump — to be as familiar with me as my dog; and he insists on being formal and reminding me of his rank — look how he writes."

He gave Poins the letter, and Poins read out loud, "John Falstaff, knight."

Poins then commented, "He reminds everyone that he is a knight as often as he has opportunity. He is like men who are kin to the King: Every time they prick their finger, they say, 'There's some of the King's blood spilt.' Someone who pretends not to know what they meant asks, 'How is that?' The answer is as ready as a borrower is ready to hold out his hat for a lender to place money in it: 'I am the King's poor cousin, sir.'"

"True," Prince Hal said. "They will be kin to us, even if they have to trace their kinship all the way back to Japhet, the Biblical ancestor of all Europeans."

He took the letter from Poins and read out loud: "Sir John Falstaff, knight, to the son of the King, nearest his father, Harry Prince of Wales, greeting."

Poins said, "Why, this is written as if Falstaff were a King addressing his inferiors. In ordinary letters, the name of the person being written to comes before that of the writer."

"Quiet!" Prince Hal said. He then read out loud, "I will imitate the honorable Romans in brevity."

Poins said, "He must mean brevity in breath — being short-winded. His letter is wordy."

Prince Hal read out loud, "I commend me to you, I commend you, and I leave you."

Falstaff was imitating Julius Caesar's "I came, I saw, I conquered." He meant this: I present my regards to you, I approve of you, and I say goodbye to you.

Prince Hal continued reading the letter out loud: "Be not too familiar with Poins; for he misuses your favors so much that he swears that you will marry Nell, his sister. Repent at idle times as you may; and so, farewell. Yours, by yea and no, which is as much as to say, as you use him — I return good for good, and ill for ill. I am JACK FALSTAFF with my familiars, JOHN with my brothers and sisters, and SIR JOHN with all Europe."

Poins said, "My lord, I'll soak this letter in wine and make him eat it."

Prince Hal said, "If you do, you will make him eat twenty of his words. But do you say this about me, Ned? Am I to marry your sister?"

Poins said, "I wish that God would send my sister no worse fortune than that! But I never said that you would marry my sister."

"Well, thus we play fools by wasting the time, and the spirits of the wise — the angels — sit in the clouds and mock us for being so wasteful," Prince Hal said.

He asked Bardolph, "Is Falstaff, your master, here in London?"

"Yes, my lord."

"Where does he eat his meals? Does the old boar feed in the old, usual sty?"

"He eats at the old place, my lord, in Eastcheap."

"With whom does he eat?

The page replied, "With Ephesians, my lord, of the old church."

These "Ephesians" were his boon companions. These "Ephesians" resembled the Ephesians of the New Testament before their conversion; they frequently indulged in wine.

"Do any women dine with him?" Prince Hal asked.

"None, my lord, but old Mistress Quickly and Mistress Doll Tearsheet," the page replied.

"What pagan may she be?" Prince Hal asked. He was referring to Doll Tearsheet because he already knew Mistress Quickly. He also knew that any woman who dined with Falstaff would likely not be known for Christian virtue.

The page identified both women, referring first to Mistress Quickly: "A proper gentlewoman, sir, and a kinswoman of my master's."

"Kinswoman, huh?" Prince Hal said. "She will be such kin as the parish heifers are to the town bull."

The town bull, which was kept at the expense of the parish or town, was used to service — that is, impregnate — many cows.

Prince Hal asked Poins, "Shall we sneak upon them, Ned, while they are eating supper?"

"I am your shadow, my lord," Poins said. "I will follow you."

Prince Hal said, "You, boy, and you, Bardolph, don't tell Falstaff that I have returned to London. Here is some money to pay you for your silence."

He gave them some money, and Bardolph said, "I have no tongue, sir."

The page added, "And as for mine, sir, I will keep it silent about this topic."

"Fare you well," Prince Hal said. "You may go now."

Bardolph and the page left.

Prince Hal said, "This Doll Tearsheet must be a prostitute who is as commonly used as a road."

"I will bet you that she is as commonly used as the heavily travelled road between Saint Alban's and London," Poins said.

Prince Hal asked Poins, "How can we see Falstaff tonight in his true colors, acting the way he really acts in accordance with his true nature, and not have him recognize us?"

"We can put on two leather jackets and aprons, the kind that tapsters wear, and wait upon him at his table as his tapsters."

"Jove, King of the gods of men, transformed himself from a god to a bull in order to run away with and sleep with the mortal woman Europa. That transformation was a serious declension. Now I will transform myself from a Prince to an apprentice tapster. That is a low transformation! I shall do this folly because I have a fun purpose for doing it. In everything the purpose must counterbalance the folly."

He added, "Follow me, Ned," and they left.

At Warkworth, in front of the castle of the Earl of Northumberland, the Earl himself and his wife, Lady Northumberland, were talking. With them was Lady Percy, the widow of Hotspur, Northumberland's son. He had died during the Battle of Shrewsbury, in part because the reinforcements that he had expected from his father had not shown up. Hotspur ended up fighting with an army that was much smaller than he had expected to fight with.

Northumberland said, "Please, loving wife, and gentle daughter-in-law, support me as I do what I must do, difficult as it may be. Do not look troubled. These troubled times are already too troublesome to me."

His wife, Lady Northumberland, replied, "I give up. I will speak no more. Do what you will; let your wisdom be your guide."

"Sweet wife, my honor has been pawned, and the only way for me to redeem my honor is to go to war."

Lady Percy, Hotspur's widow, said, "For God's sake, do not go and fight in this rebellion! The time was, father-in-law, that you broke your word, when you were more bound to it than now. Your own son, my heart's dear Hotspur, threw many a look northward, hoping to see his father bring his army, but he longed in vain for the reinforcements you were supposed to bring to him. Who then persuaded you to stay at home? At the Battle of Shrewsbury, two honors were lost: yours and your son's. Your son also lost his life. As for your honor, may the God of Heaven brighten it! As for Hotspur's honor, it stuck upon him like the Sun is stuck in the blue vault of the sky, and Hotspur's light moved all the chivalry of England to do brave acts: He was indeed the mirror that the noble youth used to dress themselves: They imitated him. Everyone except those who had no legs imitated the way that Hotspur walked. Hotspur spoke loudly and quickly and his words were thickly gathered together. This was a blemish in his speech, but valiant youth imitated his speech. Those who could speak low and slowly would abuse their own perfect speech so that they would seem like Hotspur. In speech, in gait, in diet, in recreations, in military rules, in temperament, he was the target and mirror, example, and rulebook that others imitated.

"And Hotspur — oh, wondrous Hotspur! Oh, miracle of men! You left Hotspur, who was second to none, without reinforcements and without support from you. Hotspur looked upon the hideous god of war when he, Hotspur, was at a disadvantage and had to fight from a position of weakness. He had to fight in a battlefield where nothing but the sound of Hotspur's name seemed to be able to stand up against Henry IV's forces. You left him, and you allowed him to do this.

"Never — oh, never — do Hotspur's ghost the wrong to value your honor with others as being more valuable than your honor with him. Let the others fight alone! The Lord Marshal Mowbray and the Archbishop of York are strong: Had my sweet Hotspur had but half their number of soldiers, today might I, hanging on Hotspur's neck, have talked about Prince Hal's grave."

Northumberland said, "Damn, fair daughter-in-law, you dishearten me by newly lamenting ancient oversights. But I must go and meet with danger by fighting with the troops of the Lord Marshal Mowbray and the Archbishop of York, or danger will seek me in another place and find me less prepared to defend myself against it."

His wife advised, "Flee to Scotland, and wait until the noble rebels and the armed common soldiers have gotten a little taste of their strength in battle."

Lady Percy agreed that that was a good plan: "If they gain ground against and get the advantage of the King, then you can join with them, like a rib of steel, to make their strength stronger; but if you love us, first let them fight by themselves without your reinforcements. Your son, Hotspur, did that. You allowed him to do that. That is how I became a widow. I shall never live long enough to shed enough tears upon rosemary, the plant of remembrance, to make it grow and sprout as high as Heaven, and be the memorial that my noble husband deserves."

Northumberland said, "Come, come, go in with me. My mind is like a tide that has reached its full height and neither wanes nor waxes: It is at a standstill, running neither way. Eagerly would I go to meet the Archbishop of York and his troops, but many thousand reasons hold me back. I will go to Scotland and stay there until the right time and the right opportunity for me to fight present themselves."

At the Boar's Head Tavern in Eastcheap, two drawers, aka tapsters or bartenders, were talking. They were preparing a room for the arrival of Sir John Falstaff and others.

The first drawer said, "What the Devil have you brought there? Apple-johns? You know that Sir John cannot endure an apple-john."

Apple-johns were apples that were eaten after they had become shriveled and withered. Saint John's Day was June 24, and the apples, which were harvested after that date, kept until then.

"By the Mass, you are saying the truth," the second drawer said. "Prince Hal once set a dish of apple-johns in front of Falstaff, and told him here were five more Sir Johns, and, putting off his hat, the Prince said, 'I will now take my leave of these six dry, round, old, withered knights.' It angered Falstaff to the heart, but he got over it and has forgotten it."

"Why, then, cover the table with a cloth, and set the apple-johns down," the first drawer said, "and see if you can locate Sneak's noise; Mistress Tearsheet would like to hear some music."

A group of geese on the ground is a gaggle. A group of hens is a brood. A noise of musicians is a band.

He continued, "Hurry! The room where they dined is too hot; they'll come in here soon."

The second drawer replied, "Also coming in here soon will be the Prince and Master Poins. They will put on two of our jackets and aprons. Sir John must not know about it. Bardolph told me this."

"By the Mass, here will be good times," the first drawer said. "It will be an excellent joke and like the eighth day of a festival."

"I'll see if I can find Sneak," the second drawer said, and then both drawers departed.

Mistress Quickly and Doll Tearsheet entered the room. Doll Tearsheet's name suited her; she was a prostitute.

Mistress Quickly said to Doll Tearsheet, who had been ill, "Truly, sweetheart, I think now that you are in an excellent good temporality [temper]: your pulsidge [pulse] beats as extraordinarily as any heart would desire; and your color, I warrant you, is as red as any rose, truly! But, truly, you have drunk too much canaries [wine from the Canary Islands]; and that's a marvelously intoxicating wine, and it perfumes [pervades] the blood before one can say, 'What's this?' How do you feel now?"

"Better than I did," Doll Tearsheet said, and then she coughed.

"Why, that's well said," Mistress Quickly said. "A good heart is worth gold. Look, here comes Sir John."

Falstaff entered the room, singing, "When Arthur first in court."

He called, "Empty the jordan. Empty the chamberpot!"

Then he sang, "And was a worthy King."

He asked, "How are you now, Mistress Doll?"

Mistress Quickly replied, "Sick of a calm, truly."

She meant "qualm," but Falstaff pretended that she really had meant "calm."

"So is all her sect," Falstaff said. "Anytime a prostitute is in a calm and not furiously working, they are sick."

Doll Tearsheet said, "You muddy rascal, is that all the comfort you give me?"

"You make fat rascals, Mistress Doll. You make rascals fat."

"I make them fat! Gluttony and diseases make them fat; I do not make them fat."

"If the cook helps to make gluttony, then you help to make the diseases, Doll. We catch venereal diseases from you, Doll. We catch them from you. Grant that, my poor virtue, grant that."

"You do the catching," Doll Tearsheet replied. "You catch at and steal our necklaces and other jewelry."

Falstaff sang, "Your brooches, pearls, and gems."

He then said, "All of the 'jewels' we receive from such as you are sores on our genitals. People who serve bravely in battle limp off the battlefield. Those of us who use your services come away from the breach in your wall — the opening in your body — with our pikes bravely bent. We then bravely go to the doctor to get our venereal disease cured, and then we again bravely mount our attack and discharge our weapons against you —"

Doll Tearsheet said, "Go hang yourself, you muddy conger eel, go hang yourself!"

"Truly," Mistress Quickly said, "this happens every time you two meet. You two never meet without having an argument. You are both, truly, as rheumatic [she meant to say choleric, aka easy to anger] as two pieces of dry toast grating against each other. You cannot bear the other's conformities [infirmities]. What the Devil! One must bear, and that must be you, Doll Tearsheet. You are the weaker vessel, as they say — you are the emptier vessel."

"Can a weak empty vessel bear such a huge full barrel of a man as Falstaff?" Doll Tearsheet asked. "There is a whole cargo of Bordeaux wine in him; you have not seen a merchant ship better stuffed with a cargo of wine."

She added, "Come, I'll be friends with you, Jack. You are going to the wars; and whether I shall ever see you again or not, there is nobody who cares."

The first drawer walked into the room, which was on the second story, and said to Falstaff, "Sir, Ancient Pistol's downstairs, and he wants to speak to you."

An Ancient is a standard-bearer in the military; he is an Ensign.

Doll Tearsheet knew and loathed Pistol: "Hang him, the swaggering rascal! Don't let him in here. He is the most foul-mouthed rogue in England."

"If he is a swaggerer, let him not come in here," Mistress Quickly said. "No, by my faith. I must live among my neighbors, and I want to be on good terms with them. I'll have no swaggerers here. I have a good name and a good reputation — it is among the very best. Shut the door; there are no swaggerers allowed in here. I have not lived all this while, to have swaggering now — shut the door, please."

"Did you not hear, hostess?" Falstaff asked Mistress Quickly.

"Please, be quiet, Sir John," Mistress Quickly said. "Swaggerers are not allowed in here."

"Did you not hear? He is my Ancient."

"Tilly-fally and fiddle-faddle and fiddlesticks, Sir John," Mistress Quickly said. "Don't tell me. Your Ancient the swaggerer is not allowed inside my doors. I was made to appear before Master Tisick, the debuty [deputy] in charge of keeping the peace, the other day; and, as he said to me — it was no longer ago than last Wednesday — 'Truly, neighbor Quickly,' says he; Master Dumbe, our minister, was nearby then; 'neighbor Quickly,' says he, 'receive those who are civil because,' said he, 'you have an ill name.' He said that, and I know the reason why he said that. Says he, 'You are an honest woman, and well thought of; therefore take heed what guests you receive.' Says he, 'Receive no swaggering companions.' There comes none here. You would bless yourselves to hear what he said. No, I'll allow no swaggerers in here. I don't want any troublemakers."

Mistress Quickly had contradictory parts in her story. According to her, the deputy had told her both that she had "an ill name" and that she was "well thought of."

"He's no swaggerer, hostess," Falstaff said, "He is a tame cheater, a petty gamester who cheats a little, truly. You may stroke him as gently as a puppy greyhound. He will not even swagger with a Barbary hen, if her feathers turn back in any show of resistance."

As events would soon show, this was not true. Pistol was happy to swagger in front of a Barbary hen.

A Barbary hen is a guinea fowl; in slang, a Barbary hen is a prostitute.

Falstaff ordered, "Bring him in here, drawer."

The first drawer left to get Pistol.

"He is a cheater, you say?" Mistress Quickly asked.

She meant "escheator," or royal treasury officer. Many of them had bad reputations, and from this term we get our word "cheat."

She added, "Cheater, call you him? I will bar no honest man from my house, nor no cheater, but I do not love swaggering, to say the truth. I feel ill when I hear the word 'swagger.' Masters, feel and look at how I am shaking."

"So you are, hostess," Doll Tearsheet said.

"Am I?" Mistress Quickly said. "Yes, truly I am. I am shaking as if I were a leaf on an aspen tree. I cannot bear swaggerers."

Pistol, Bardolph, and Falstaff's page entered the room.

Pistol said loudly, "May God save you, Sir John!"

"Welcome, Ancient Pistol," Falstaff said. "Here, Pistol, I charge you with a cup of wine. I want you to discharge upon my hostess."

As you expect with Falstaff, the puns flowed like wine. "To charge" means "to drink a toast to" and "to put on a tab" and "to load a pistol." "To discharge" means "to drink a toast to another person," "to shoot," and "to ejaculate."

"I will discharge upon her, Sir John, with two bullets," Pistol replied.

The two bullets hung by his trouser-snake.

"She is Pistol-proof, sir," Falstaff replied. "You shall hardly offend her."

Mistress Quickly was beyond the age of bearing children, and she was unable to bear swaggerers such as Pistol. She said, "Come, I'll drink no proofs nor no bullets. I'll drink no more than will do me good, for no man's pleasure."

Pistol said, "Then I will charge you, Mistress Dorothy."

"Charge me!" Doll Tearsheet said. "I scorn you, scurvy fellow. What! You are a poor, base, rascally, cheating, lack-linen mate! You own very few shirts. Go away, you moldy rogue, go away! I am meet for Falstaff, your master."

Anyone hearing Doll Tearsheet might think that she had said that she was meat for Falstaff rather than meet, aka fitting.

"I know you, Mistress Dorothy," Pistol said. "I know all about you."

"Go away, you cut-purse, pickpocketing rascal!" Doll Tearsheet shouted.

She pulled out a knife and said, "You filthy purse-snatcher, go away! I swear by this wine, I'll thrust my knife in your moldy cheeks, if you try to play saucy tricks on me. Go away, you bottle-ale, boozy rascal! You are a basket-hilt stale juggler, you! I don't even think you fight with a real sword — you fight with a wooden cudgel that has a hilt made of strips of metal woven like a basket. You are like a performer fighting with wooden cudgels as entertainment at a country fair! Since when are you good enough for me, I ask you, sir? By God's light, you have two points on your shoulder! Are those laces for securing armor or have you sewn together two handkerchiefs to make yourself a half-shirt?"

"May God not let me live unless I murder your ruff for this!" Pistol shouted.

Prostitutes such as Doll Tearsheet wore a large ruff — a projecting starched frill — around their neck. Drunken bullies sometimes tore these ruffs and assaulted the prostitutes.

"No more of this, Pistol," Falstaff said, and then he punned "I would not have you go off in here. Discharge yourself of our company, Pistol."

"Good Captain Pistol," Mistress Quickly said, giving him a military title he had not earned, "do not go off in here, sweet Captain."

"Captain!" Doll Tearsheet exclaimed.

She said to Pistol, "You abominable damned cheater, aren't you ashamed to be called Captain? If Captains were of my mind, they would truncheon you out of their ranks — they would beat you with a truncheon for taking their title before you have earned it. You a Captain! You slave, for what action have you earned that title? For tearing a poor whore's ruff in a bawdy house?"

She continued, "He a Captain! Hang him — he is a rogue! He lives upon moldy stewed prunes and day-old cakes that he gets at bawdy houses and pastry-cook shops. A Captain! By God's light, these villains will make the word 'Captain' as odious as the word 'occupy,' which was an excellent word before it was used to refer to fornication. Therefore, real Captains need to make sure that people such as Pistol do not steal the title of Captain."

Falstaff was a real Captain.

"Please, go downstairs and leave, good Ancient," Bardolph said to Pistol.

"Listen to me, Mistress Doll," Falstaff said.

Pistol shouted, "Leave! Not I! I tell you what, Corporal Bardolph, I could tear Doll Tearsheet to pieces! I'll be revenged on her!"

"Please, go downstairs and leave," the page said to Pistol.

"I'll see her damned first!" Pistol shouted. He loved extravagant language of the kind he heard in action-filled plays. "She shall be damned to the Underworld, to Pluto's damned lake, by this hand, to the infernal deep, with Erebus and tortures vile, also. Hold hook and line, say I. Down, down, dogs! Down, traitors! Have we not Hiren here?"

Hiren was a woman's name that Pistol had given to his sword, possibly because his sword was made of iron.

"Good Captain Peesel [Pistol], be quiet," Mistress Quickly pleaded. "It is very late, truly: I beseek [beseech] you now, aggravate [she meant to say "moderate"] your choler [anger]."

Pistol loved extravagant language so much that he did not care if it made sense or was appropriate to the situation. He shouted, "These be good humors, indeed! Shall packhorses and hollow pampered jades of Asia, which cannot travel but thirty miles each day, compare with Caesars, and with Cannibals, and with Trojant Greeks? Nay, rather damn them with King Cerberus; and let the welkin roar."

Pistol sometimes mixed up his literary references. Cerberus was not a King; Cerberus was the three-headed dog that served as a guard dog in Hell. When referring to the "hollow pampered jades of Asia" and how much they could travel in a day, he was misquoting some lines from Christopher Marlowe's play *Tamburlaine, Part 2* — according to that play, the jades [actually, two conquered kings drawing his chariot] could draw a chariot only twenty miles a day. His reference to Cannibals may have been a mistake for Hannibals;

Hannibal was the great Carthaginian general who crossed the Alps with his elephants to make war on the Romans in Italy. Apparently, by "Trojant Greeks," he meant the Greeks who besieged Troy.

Pistol continued, "Shall we fall foul for toys? Shall we fight over toys?"

He was referring to Doll Tearsheet.

Mistress Quickly said, "Truly, Captain, these are very bitter words."

"Leave here, good Ancient," Bardolph said. "This will grow into a brawl soon."

"Die men like dogs! Give crowns like pins! Have we not Hiren here?"

When Pistol shouted, "Give crowns like pins!" he was thinking of Tamburlaine, who gave away Kingdoms as if they were valueless pins.

Mistress Quickly misunderstood the word "Hiren," which was the name of Pistol's sword. She thought that he was referring to a woman — probably a prostitute — whom he believed was at the tavern.

"On my word, Captain," she said, "there's no such woman here. What the Devil? Do you think that I would deny she was here if she really was here? For God's sake, be quiet."

"Then feed, and be fat, my fair Calipolis!" Pistol shouted. "Come, give me some wine. *Si fortune me tormente, sperato me contento.*"

The motto's garbled Spanish and Italian meant, "If fortune torments me, hope comforts me."

He continued, "Fear we broadsides? No, let the fiend give fire. Give me some wine." He placed his sword on a table and said, "Sweetheart, lie you there. Come we to full points here; and are etceteras no thing?"

A full point is a period at the end of a sentence. Pistol was saying, "Have we come to an end here? Are we done shouting?"

Pistol could be bawdy. A "thing" is a penis, which has a point. By "etceteras," he meant vaginas. An etcetera is no thing.

"Pistol, I wish that you would be quiet," Falstaff said.

"Sweet knight, I kiss your fist," Pistol said. "What! We have seen the seven stars."

This was true. Falstaff and Pistol had seen the seven stars of the Big Dipper together. They had stayed up late at night.

"For God's sake, throw him downstairs," Doll Tearsheet said. "I cannot endure such a worthless rascal."

"Throw him — me! — downstairs! Know we not Galloway nags?"

Galloway nags were small high-stepping horses bred in Ireland. A nag was also slang for a prostitute. Doll Tearsheet's job was to be ridden.

"Quoit him down, Bardolph, and while you are at it, quiet him down, Bardolph," Falstaff said. "Quoit him down like a shove-groat shilling."

"To quoit him down" meant to throw him downstairs. A quoit was an iron ring that was thrown in a game similar to horseshoes. A shove-groat shilling was used as a puck in a game similar to shuffleboard.

Falstaff added, "If Pistol does nothing but speak nothing, he shall be nothing here. He is talking nonsense, and I will not allow him to stay here."

"Come, let's get you downstairs," Bardolph said to Pistol.

"What!" Pistol shouted. "Shall we make incisions in each other's bodies? Shall we imbrue our blades with blood?"

He grabbed his sword and said, "Then death rock me asleep; abridge and shorten my doleful days! Why, then, let grievous, ghastly, gaping wounds untwine the Sisters Three! Come, Atropos, I say!"

The Three Sisters are the Three Fates. Clotho spun the thread of life. Lachesis measured the string of life. Atropos cut the thread of life; when she cut your thread of life, you died. "To untwine" means to remove by unwinding. Grievous, ghastly, gaping wounds might untwine the thread of life and get it cut, but they would never untwine the Sisters Three.

"Here's 'goodly' stuff coming!" Mistress Quickly said. "This fight will be bad for the reputation of my tavern!"

"Give me my rapier, boy," Falstaff said.

The page handed Falstaff his sword, which was in a sheath.

"Please, Jack," Doll Tearsheet said. "Please do not draw your sword."

She liked — even loved — him, and she did not want him to get hurt.

Falstaff drew his sword and said to Pistol, "Get yourself downstairs."

Mistress Quickly said, "Here's a 'goodly' tumult! I'll forswear keeping a tavern, before I'll be in these tirrits [terrors and fits] and frights. Murder! I can just see it happening now! Heavens! Put up your naked weapons! Put up your naked weapons!"

Pistol was no fighter. After Falstaff and he exchanged a few thrusts of their swords, he fled. Bardolph pursued him downstairs and out of the tavern.

Falstaff pretended to continue to fight with his sword.

"Please, Jack, relax and be quiet," Doll Tearsheet said, putting away her knife. "The rascal's gone. Ah, you whoreson little valiant villain, you!"

Mistress Quickly asked Falstaff, "Did he hurt you in the groin? I thought he made a shrewd thrust at your belly."

Bardolph returned, and Falstaff asked him, "Have you thrown him out of doors?"

"Yes, sir," Bardolph said. "The rascal's drunk. You have wounded him, sir, in the shoulder."

"He is a rascal!" Falstaff said. "I can't believe that he dared to challenge me! I am his superior officer, and he should have left the first time I told him to!"

"Ah, you sweet little rogue, you!" Doll Tearsheet said. "Oh, poor ape, how you are sweating! Come, let me wipe your face; come on, you whoreson fat-cheeks! Oh, you are a rogue! Truly, I love you: You are as valorous as Hector of Troy, you are worth five of Agamemnon, and you are ten times better than the Nine Worthies. Oh, you are a villain!"

This was high praise. Hector was the leader of the Trojans in the Trojan War. He was the bravest Trojan, and when he died, everyone knew that Troy was doomed to fall to the Greeks. Agamemnon was the leader of the Greeks in the Trojan War. The Nine Worthies were nine heroes: three were pagan, three were Jewish, and three were Christian. The three pagan heroes were Hector, Alexander the Great, and Julius Caesar. The three Jewish heroes were Joshua, David, and Judas Maccabaeus. The three Christian heroes were King Arthur, Holy Roman Emperor Charlemagne, and Godfrey of Bouillon, who was one of the leaders of the First Crusade.

"Pistol is a rascally slave!" Falstaff said. "I will toss the rogue in a blanket."

This was regarded as a suitable punishment for a coward.

Doll Tearsheet replied, "Do it, if you dare to risk your life. If you do it, I will toss you between a pair of sheets."

She regarded this as a suitable reward for her hero.

Sneak and some other musicians entered the room.

Seeing them, the page said to Falstaff, "The music has come, sir."

"Let them play," Falstaff said.

He said to the musicians, "Play, sirs," and then he requested, "Sit on my knee, Doll."

She sat on his knee, and the musicians began playing.

Falstaff added, "Pistol is a rascally bragging slave! The rogue fled from me like quicksilver — like Mercury, the fleet messenger of the gods!"

Doll Tearsheet said, "Truly, he did."

She joked, "And you followed him as quickly as if you were a church building."

She added, more seriously, "You whoreson little tidy Bartholomew boar-pig, when will you stop fighting during the days and thrusting during the nights, and when will you begin to patch up your old body for Heaven?"

A Bartholomew boar-pig was a roast pig served at the Bartholomew Fair, which was held in London annually on August 24.

"Please, good Doll," Falstaff requested, "please do not speak to me as if you were a death's-head, a skull, a *memento mori*, a reminder that one day we will die. Please do not ask me to think about my death."

Prince Hal and Poins entered the room; they were wearing the jackets and aprons of drawers to hide their identities.

Doll Tearsheet recognized them and knew that they wanted to play a joke on Falstaff, their sometimes companion.

Doll Tearsheet asked Falstaff, "What is Prince Hal like?"

"He is a good shallow young fellow," Falstaff replied. "He would have made a good pantryman; he would have chipped bread well."

One of the jobs of a pantryman was to chip, or cut, the burned parts off loaves of bread.

"They say Poins has a good wit," Doll Tearsheet said.

"He a good wit?" Falstaff said. "Hang him; he is a baboon! He is utterly stupid, and his wit is as thick as Tewksbury mustard. I can only wish that his wit were as sharp as the flavor of Tewksbury mustard. He has no more invention, imagination, and wit in him than a mallet or hammer has."

"Why does the Prince regard Poins as a good friend, then?"

"Because their legs are both of an attractive quality and look good in stockings, and because he plays a good game of quoits, and because he eats conger eels — which are reputed to make eaters stupid — seasoned with fennel. Poins has a good appetite and a dull wit. In addition, he is good at drinking games. If you float some small pieces of lit candles in an alcoholic beverage, he can manage to drink the alcohol without being badly burnt. He is also able to play boyish games well, and to become boisterous and jump up on bar stools, and he swears with a good talent, and he wears his boots very tight to show off his attractive legs, which are like the boots and legs on a sign that advertises a boot maker. He also breeds no anger when he tells his discreet stories — he does not tell secrets. He has other playful qualities that show that he has a weak mind and an able body. Because of these qualities, Prince Hal allows Poins to be in his presence. Prince Hal is just like Poins. If you put them in a pair of scales, the scales would be exactly even."

Prince Hal whispered to Poins, "Shouldn't this nave of a wheel have his ears cut off?"

The nave of a wheel is the round hub of a wheel. Having one's ears cut off was the punishment for defaming a member of the royal family.

"Let's beat him in front of his whore," Poins said.

"Look," Prince Hal said. "The withered elder is getting his poll clawed like a parrot."

Doll Tearsheet was scratching the top of Falstaff's head.

"Is it not strange that sexual desire should by so many years outlive sexual performance?" Poins asked.

He believed that Falstaff, because of his advanced age and immense obesity, was impotent.

"Kiss me, Doll," Falstaff requested.

She obliged.

"Saturn and Venus are this year in conjunction!" Prince Hal said. "I wonder what the almanac says about that!"

Saturn was the planet of old age, and Venus was the planet of love. If Poins were wrong about Falstaff being impotent, it seemed that soon Saturn and Venus, aka Falstaff and Doll Tearsheet, would be in conjunction. Almanacs then and now concern themselves with astrology.

"And look, the fiery Trigon, Falstaff's man, is lisping words of love to his master's old tables, his notebook, his counsel-keeper, his confidant, his keeper of secrets," Poins said. "To speak plainly, fiery-faced Bardolph is whispering sweet nothings to Mistress Quickly."

The signs of the Zodiac are divided into four groups of three, each of which is called a Trigon. Each Trigon is associated with water, air, earth, or fire. The three astrological signs associated with fire are Aries, Leo, and Sagittarius.

"You are giving me flattering kisses," Falstaff said.

"Truly, I kiss you with a most constant and faithful heart," Doll Tearsheet replied.

"I am old. I am old," Falstaff mourned.

"I love you better than I love any scurvy young boy."

"Of which material do you want a kirtle made?" Falstaff asked. "I shall receive money on Thursday. I will give you a cap tomorrow."

A woman wore a kirtle between her petticoats and her gown.

The musicians were still playing, and Falstaff said, "This is a merry song. Come, it is growing late; let's go to bed."

He paused and then said to Doll Tearsheet, "You'll forget me when I am gone."

He may have been talking about going to war; he may have been talking about dying.

"Truly, you'll make me cry, if you say that," Doll Tearsheet replied, "I will not dress in fine clothing until you return from the war. Well, wait and see. We will see what will happen."

"Bring us some wine, Francis," Falstaff said to Prince Hal, who was pretending to be a drawer. Francis was one of the drawers at the Boar's Head Tavern.

Prince Hal responded the way that a drawer would: "Anon, anon, sir. Right away, right away, sir."

He then came forward and faced Falstaff so that Falstaff could recognize him. Poins did the same thing.

Falstaff, who did recognize them, said, "Ha! Are you a bastard son of the King's? And aren't you Poins' brother?"

"Why, you globe of sinful continents!" Prince Hal said. "You are a huge and round mass of sinful contents! What a life you lead!"

"I lead a better life than you," Falstaff said. "I am a gentleman; you are a drawer."

"Very true, sir," Prince Hal said, "and I come to draw you out of this room by your ears."

"Oh, may the Lord preserve your good grace!" Mistress Quickly said. "Truly, welcome to London. Now, may the Lord bless that sweet face of yours! Oh, have you come from Wales?"

Falstaff said to Prince Hal, "You whoreson mad compound of majesty," and then he added, referring to Doll Tearsheet, "by this light flesh and corrupt blood, you are welcome."

A light woman was a woman who engaged in fornication.

"You fat fool!" Doll Tearsheet shouted, getting off Falstaff's lap. "I scorn you!"

Poins said to Prince Hal, "My lord, he will drive you out of your mood for getting revenge on him for what he said about you, and he will turn everything into a merry joke, unless you strike while the iron is hot."

Prince Hal said to Falstaff, "You whoreson candle-mine, you mine of tallow fat, you! How vilely did you speak of me just now before this honest, virtuous, civil gentlewoman!"

"May God bless your good heart!" Mistress Quickly said. "She really is an honest, virtuous, civil gentlewoman!"

"Did you hear what I said about you?" Falstaff asked Prince Hal.

"Yes, I did, and I am sure that you will say that you recognized me although I was in disguise, as you did when you ran away following the robbery at Gad's Hill. You will say this: You recognized me just now, and you said those bad things about me on purpose just to test my patience."

"No, no, no," Falstaff said. "That is not true; I did not think you were within hearing distance."

"I shall drive you then to confess that you willfully showered words of abuse on me," Prince Hal said, "and then I will know how to handle you and what punishment to give to you."

"There was no abuse, Hal," Falstaff said. "On my honor, there was no abuse."

"You claim that you did not insult me and call me a pantryman and a bread-chipper and I know not what else?"

"There was no abuse, Hal."

"No abuse?" Ned Poins asked.

"No abuse, Ned, in the world," Falstaff said. "Honest Ned, there was none. I dispraised Prince Hal before the wicked, so that the wicked might not fall in love with him. By so doing, I have done the part of a careful friend and a true subject, and Hal's father the King ought to give me thanks for it. So, you can see that there was no abuse, Hal. There was none, Ned, none. No, truly, boys, there was none."

"Let us see now," Prince Hal said, "whether your pure fear and entire cowardice has made you wrong this virtuous gentlewoman so you can make peace with us. Is she — this woman who was just now sitting on your lap — one of the wicked? Is your hostess here — Mistress Quickly — one of the wicked? Is the boy who is your page one of the wicked? Or honest Bardolph, whose zeal can be seen burning in his nose — Puritans praise burning zeal — one of the wicked?"

"Answer him, you dead elm-tree trunk, answer him," Poins said.

"The fiend we know as Satan has written Bardolph's name among those whose souls are irrecoverable," Falstaff said. "His red face is Lucifer's kitchen, aka Hell, where he does nothing but roast malt-worms — alcoholics. As for the boy, there is a good angel about him, but the Devil has blinded the boy so that he cannot see the good angel."

"What about the women?" Prince Hal asked.

"As for one of them, she is in Hell already, and she burns poor souls."

Falstaff was referring to Doll Tearsheet, who infected men with venereal disease and made them burn when they urinated.

"As for the other, I owe her money, and whether she has been damned for that, I don't know."

"I have not been damned for that, I assure you," Mistress Quickly said.

"I think that you are right and you have not been damned for that," Falstaff said. "I think you have avoided being damned for that."

Puritans regarded the lending of money — usury — as a sin. But since Falstaff had no intention of paying back the money he had borrowed from Mistress Quickly, was she really engaging in usury?

Falstaff continued, "But by Mother Mary, there is another indictment against Mistress Quickly."

He said to her, "You allow flesh to be sold and consumed in your house, contrary to the law; for which sin I think you will howl in Hell."

Eating houses were not allowed by law to serve meat during Lent.

Mistress Quickly said, "All keepers of eating houses do that; what's a joint of mutton or two in a whole Lent?"

Falstaff had in mind a different kind of selling and consuming flesh; he was referring to the flesh of prostitutes. "Mutton" was a slang word used to refer to prostitutes.

Prince Hal said to Doll Tearsheet, "You, gentlewoman —"

He hesitated.

Doll Tearsheet asked, "What do you want, your grace?"

Falstaff said, "His grace says that which his flesh rebels against."

He was punning again. He knew that Prince Hal knew that Doll Tearsheet was not a gentlewoman. One meaning of Falstaff's sentence was that Prince Hal was saying something that he knew was not true. Another meaning was that as Prince Hal called Doll Tearsheet a gentlewoman, a part of his body that knew what she really was, was rebelling in an uprising — that is, rising up (and becoming erect).

Knocking sounded on the door downstairs.

"Who is knocking so loudly?" Mistress Quickly said. "Go and see who is at the door, Francis."

Peto, another of Prince Hal's Eastcheap friends, walked upstairs.

Prince Hal saw him and said, "Peto, how are you! What news have you brought to me?"

Peto replied, "The King, your father, is at Westminster. Twenty weak and weary messengers have come from the North with important news, and as I was coming here, I met and overtook a dozen Captains, who were bare headed, sweating, knocking at the tavern doors, and asking everyone for the location of Sir John Falstaff."

"By Heaven, Poins," Prince Hal said, "I feel myself much to blame, so idly to profane and waste the precious time. Now a storm of war, like the South wind blowing black clouds, begins to melt and drop tears upon our bare unhelmeted heads. Bring me my sword and cloak."

He then said, "Falstaff, good night."

Prince Hal, Poins, Peto, and Bardolph left the room.

Falstaff said, "Now comes in the sweetest morsel of the night, and we must go from here and leave it unpicked."

Knocking sounded on the door downstairs.

Bardolph came into the room and Falstaff said to him, "What's the matter?"

Bardolph replied, "You must leave here and go to court, sir, immediately; a dozen Captains are waiting at the door for you."

Falstaff said, "Pay the musicians."

He then said, "Farewell, hostess; farewell, Doll. You see, my good wenches, how men of merit are sought after. The undeserver may sleep when the man of action is called on to go to work. Farewell, good wenches. If I am not sent away to war immediately, I will see you again before I go."

"I cannot speak," Doll Tearsheet said. "My heart is ready to burst. Well, sweet Jack, take care of yourself."

"Farewell, farewell," he said.

Falstaff and Bardolph went downstairs.

Mistress Quickly said as Falstaff left, "Well, fare you well. I have known you these past twenty-nine years, come peascod-time — come the time when the pods form peas. But an honester and truer-hearted man — well, fare you well."

Bardolph called from downstairs, "Mistress Tearsheet!"

"What's the matter?" Mistress Quickly called back.

Bardolph called, "Good Mistress Tearsheet, come to Falstaff, my master."

Mistress Quickly, who had gone to the door of the room, said, "Oh, run, Doll, run; run, good Doll. Come."

Crying with sadness at Falstaff's departure, Doll Tearsheet stood up.

Mistress Quickly repeated, "Come, Doll."

Doll Tearsheet ran downstairs.

Say what you will about Falstaff, at least two women loved him.

# CHAPTER 3

## — 3.1 —

In a room of the palace at Westminster at night, King Henry IV, wearing night clothing, said to his young servant, "Go and call the Earls of Surrey and of Warwick to come to me, but tell them to read these letters and carefully consider their content before they come. Hurry."

His young servant left to do the errands.

King Henry IV said to himself, "How many thousands of my poorest subjects are at this hour asleep! Sleep, gentle Sleep, Nature's soft nurse, how have I so frightened you that you will no longer weigh my eyelids down and steep my senses in forgetfulness? Why, Sleep, do you prefer to lie in smoky hovels, stretching yourself upon uncomfortable straw mattresses and being sung to by buzzing night insects as you go to your slumber, rather than to lie in the perfumed chambers of the nobility, under costly canopies, and lulled to slumber with the sound of sweetest melodies?

"Oh, you dull god, why do you lie with the lowly born in loathsome beds, and allow me, the King, to lie in my Kingly bed as if I were the mechanism in a watch case? The mechanism keeps on moving and is ready to raise an alarm, but the watch case is still and does not move.

"Sleep, you seal shut the eyes of the ship-boy who is in the crow's nest at the top of the high and giddy mast, although his brains are rocked by the rude imperious surge of a tossing sea and by the visitation of the winds that take the ruffian waves by their tops, curling their monstrous heads and hanging them with such a deafening clamor in the slippery clouds that the noise wakes up Death itself.

"How can you, partial Sleep, give your repose to the wet sea-boy in an hour so rude and violent and noisy, and yet in the calmest and stillest night deny your repose to a King who has everything that is needed to make Sleep comfortable?

"Then happy lowly born, lie down! Uneasy lies the head that wears a crown."

Warwick and Surrey entered the room.

"May your majesty enjoy many happy mornings!" Warwick said.

"Is it morning, lords?" King Henry IV asked.

"It is past one o'clock," Warwick said.

"Why, then, good morning to you all, my lords. Have you read over the letters that I sent you?"

"We have, my liege," Warwick replied.

"Then you perceive how foul the body of our Kingdom is. You understand with what danger rank diseases grow near the heart of our Kingdom. You understand how serious the rebellion is."

"The Kingdom is like a body that is ill, but that can be restored to its former health with good advice and a little medicine," Warwick said. "My Lord Northumberland will soon be cooled and his rebellion stopped."

"I wish to God that I could read the Book of Fate, and see the passage of time and the process of change that make mountains level, and the continent, which becomes weary of solid firmness, melt itself into the sea! And I would like to see, at other times, how the beaches grow and become so big that tides can no longer wash over them. The beaches are the belt of the sea-god Neptune, and they can grow until they become too large for his hips and so parts of the beaches are no longer touched by sea-tides. I would like to see the ironic tricks played by chance occurrences upon men, and how changes fill the cup of alteration with many different liquors!

"If it were possible to see these things in a book, the happiest youth, viewing the course of his life — what perils he would encounter, and what crosses he would bear — would shut the book and then sit down and die.

"Not ten years have passed since Richard II and the Earl of Northumberland, who were then great friends, feasted together. Two years after they were feasting together, they were at war against each other. Only eight years ago, Northumberland was the man nearest my soul. Like a brother, he toiled for me and he laid his love and life under my foot — he submitted himself to me. For my sake, he even defied King Richard II.

"But which of you was there? If I remember correctly, you were present, Warwick, when Richard II, with his eyes brimful of tears, rebuked and berated by Northumberland, spoke these words that are now proved to be a prophecy: 'Northumberland, you are the ladder by which my cousin Henry Bolingbroke — King Henry IV — ascends to my throne.'

"However, God knows that I then had no such intent of ever becoming King. But necessity so bowed the state that a new King was needed, and therefore greatness and I were compelled to kiss.

"Richard II continued, 'The time shall come that foul sin, gathering head, growing to a boil and raising an army, shall break into corruption.' He continued to speak, foretelling this same time's condition and the division of our amity. He foretold that Northumberland would rebel against my rule."

"There is a history in all men's lives," Warwick replied, "that tells what happened in the past. Observing the past, a man may identify with a high degree of accuracy the things that are most likely to happen. These things that have not yet occurred have their seeds and weak beginnings stored in the past as if they were in a treasury.

"Such things hatch and become the brood of time. And by knowing the necessary pattern of cause and effect, King Richard II might create a guess — which turned out to be accurate — that great Northumberland, who was then false to him, would from that seed grow to a greater falseness that could find no ground to take root upon, except on you."

"Are these things then necessities?" King Henry IV asked. "Then let us meet them like necessities although that same word 'necessities' cries out against us. I hate to think that these things had to happen.

"They say the Archbishop of York and the Earl of Northumberland have an army of fifty thousand soldiers."

"That cannot be, my lord," Warwick replied. "Rumor does double, like the voice and echo, the numbers of the feared. That number is exaggerated. May it please your grace to go to bed. I swear upon my soul, my lord, that the armies that you already have sent forth shall bring this prize in very easily. Your armies shall stop the rebellion.

"To comfort you the more, let me now tell you that I have received verified information that Glendower is dead.

"Your majesty has been ill for the past two weeks, and these late hours will worsen your illness."

"I will take your advice," King Henry IV said. "Once this rebellion has been stopped, we wish, dear lords, to go on a Crusade to the Holy Land."

In front of Justice Shallow's house, Justice Shallow and Justice Silence met. A few servants were also present. The two justices were waiting for Sir John Falstaff to show up. He was headed North to fight, drafting soldiers into his company as he went.

Justice Shallow said, "Come on, come on, come on, sir. Give me your hand, sir; give me your hand, sir. You are an early riser, by the cross! And how is my good cousin Silence doing?"

Justice Silence said, "Good morning, good cousin Shallow."

"And how is my cousin, your bedfellow?" Justice Shallow said. By "bedfellow," he meant wife.

He added, "And how is your fairest daughter and mine, my goddaughter Ellen?"

"Unfortunately, she is a blackbird, cousin Shallow."

At that time in England, dark hair and dark skin were unfashionable. English men at that time preferred light hair and light skin.

"I dare say that my cousin William has become a good scholar," Justice Shallow said. "He is at Oxford still, isn't he?"

"Indeed he is, sir, to my cost."

"He must, then, be admitted to the Inns of Court to study law shortly. I was once a student at Clement's Inn, where I think they still talk of crazy Shallow."

"You were called 'lusty Shallow' then, cousin," Justice Silence said.

"Lusty" can mean lively and merry as well as filled with lust.

"By the Mass, I was called anything, and I would have done anything, too — and thoroughly and eagerly done anything, too.

"There was I, and little John Doit of Staffordshire, and black George Barnes, and Francis Pickbone, and Will Squele, a Cotswold man," Justice Shallow said.

"Shallow" is a good name for a shallow man. "Doit" is a good name for an insignificant man; a doit was a coin of very little value. "Barnes," aka barns, is a good name for a man who has country wealth. "Pickbone" is a good name for a miser. "Squele" is a good name for someone who tattles, or for someone who squeals when frightened.

Justice Shallow continued, "You will not see four such swinge-bucklers, aka swashbucklers, in all the Inns of Court again, and I may say to you, we knew where the bona-robas — the best girls — were and we had the best of them all at our beck and call. At that time Jack Falstaff, who is now Sir John, was a boy; he served as the page of Thomas Mowbray, Duke of Norfolk."

"Is he the Sir John, cousin, who is coming here soon to see about drafting soldiers?"

"He is the same Sir John, the very same," Justice Shallow said. "I saw him break Skogan's head at the court-gate, when he was a boy not thus high, and on the very same day I fought Sampson Stockfish, a fruiterer, behind Gray's Inn. Jesus, Jesus, the mad days that I have spent! And to see how many of my old acquaintances are dead!"

"We shall all follow them in death, cousin," Justice Silence said.

"That is certain, that is certain," Justice Shallow said. "Very sure, very sure. Death, as the Psalmist says, is certain to happen to us all; all of us shall die. How much does a good yoke of bullocks sell for at Stamford Fair?"

"I don't know. I was not there," Justice Silence said.

"Death is certain. Is old Double of your town still living?"

"He is dead, sir."

"Jesus, Jesus, dead!" Justice Shallow said. "He drew a good bow, and he is now dead! He shot arrows well. John of Gaunt greatly respected him and bet a lot of money on his archery prowess. Dead! He could hit a target at twelve score yards — two hundred and forty yards. He also could shoot an arrow in a straight line for fourteen score or fourteen and a half score yards — two hundred and eighty or two hundred and ninety yards. It did a man's heart good to see him do that. How much is a score of ewes now?"

"It depends on their quality," Justice Silence said. "A score of good ewes may be worth ten pounds."

"And is old Double really dead?"

Justice Silence looked up and said, "Here come two of Sir John Falstaff's men, I think."

Bardolph and another man walked up to the two justices.

Justice Shallow said, "Good morning, honest gentlemen."

Bardolph asked, "Please, which of you is Justice Shallow?"

"I am Robert Shallow, sir; I am a poor esquire of this county, and I am one of the King's justices of the peace."

An esquire was a social rank just below that of a knight.

He continued, "How can I help you?"

"My Captain, sir, commends himself to you," Bardolph replied. "My Captain, Sir John Falstaff, is a brave and valiant gentleman, by Heaven, and he is a most gallant leader."

Justice Shallow replied, "Sir John greets me well, sir. I knew him back in the day to be a good backsword man. He used to fence with a fencing stick. How is the good knight? May I ask how his wife is doing?"

"Pardon me, sir," Bardolph replied, "but a soldier is better accommodated than with a wife. Falstaff is not married."

Justice Shallow took delight in the word "accommodated," which was a new word to him.

"It is well said, truly, sir," he said, "and it is well said indeed, too. Better accommodated! It is good; yes, indeed, it is. Good phrases are surely, and ever were, very commendable. 'Accommodated!' This word comes from *accommodo*, Latin for "I adapt" or "I provide," and it is very good; it is a good phrase."

The word "accommodated" meant "supplied with" or "provided with."

"Pardon me, sir," Bardolph said. He was unsure about the meaning of the word "phrase," which meant expression. "I have heard the word. 'Phrase' you called it? By this good day, I do not know the phrase, but I will maintain the word with my sword to be a soldier-like word, and a word of exceedingly good command, by Heaven.

"Accommodated: the meaning of the word is, when a man is, as they say, accommodated; or when a man is, being, whereby he may be thought to be accommodated — which is an excellent thing."

"It is very just," Justice Shallow said.

Sir John Falstaff walked up to the group, and Justice Shallow said, "Look, here comes good Sir John. Give me your good hand, give me your worship's good hand. Truly, you are thriving well and you bear your years very well. Welcome, good Sir John."

"I am glad to see that you are well, good Master Robert Shallow," Falstaff replied. He looked at the other justice and asked, "Aren't you Master Surecard?"

"No, Sir John," Justice Shallow said. "This is my cousin Silence, who has a commission as Justice of the Peace, as do I."

"Good Master Silence," Falstaff said, "your name is very fitting for a Justice of the Peace."

"You are welcome," Justice Silence said.

Falstaff fanned himself and said, "This is hot weather, gentlemen. Have you provided me here with half a dozen fit and able men for me to look over and see if they should serve in the King's army?"

"Yes, we have, sir," Justice Shallow said. "Will you sit down?"

Falstaff replied, "Let me see them now, please."

The possible recruits walked over to them.

"Where's the roll? Where's the roll? Where's the roll?" Justice Shallow said. "Let me see, let me see, let me see. So, so. Yes, sir! Ralph Moldy! Let them come forward as I call their names; let them do so, let them do so. Let me see; where is Moldy?"

Moldy, who was on the verge of middle age, replied, "Here I am, if it please you."

"What do you think, Sir John?" Justice Shallow asked. "Isn't he a good-limbed fellow: young, strong, and from a good family?"

"Is your name Moldy?" Falstaff asked.

"Yes, if it please you."

"It is time that you were used."

"Ha, ha, ha!" Justice Shallow laughed. "That jest was most excellent, truly! Things that are moldy lack use. That was a very good jest! Truly well said, Sir John, very well said."

"Prick him," Falstaff said.

Justice Shallow was carrying a wax tablet in which the names of the possible recruits were listed. He used a stick to prick a mark by Moldy's name. That meant that Moldy had been drafted into the King's army.

Moldy complained, "I was pricked well enough before, so you could have let me alone."

He meant that he was already provided with — had been born with — a prick.

Moldy continued, "My old lady — my wife — will be undone now."

With Moldy gone to the war, his wife would have no one to "do" her.

Moldy continued, "She will have no one to do her husbandry and her drudgery."

Husbandry involves the planting of seeds. With Moldy gone to the war, his wife would have no one to plant seeds — semen — in her womb. Also, she would have no one to do the work that is less fun than the planting of those seeds.

Moldy continued, "You need not to have pricked me; there are other men fitter to go to the war than I am."

"Stop complaining," Falstaff said. "Be quiet, Moldy. You shall go to the war. Moldy, it is time that you were spent."

"Spent!" Moldy said.

"To spend" means "to ejaculate semen." It can also mean "to come to an end," which is what happens to many men's lives in wartime.

"Be quiet, fellow, be quiet," Justice Shallow said. "Stand aside. Do you know where you are and to whom you are talking?"

Moldy stepped back.

Justice Shallow paused and then he said, "As for the others, Sir John, let me see."

He looked at the roll and then called, "Simon Shadow!"

Falstaff joked, "I should draft him into the army so that I can sit under him. He is likely to be a cold soldier."

"Where's Shadow?" Justice Shallow asked.

Shadow stepped forward and said, "Here, sir."

"Shadow, whose son are you?" Falstaff asked.

"My mother's son, sir."

"Your mother's son! That is likely enough, and you are your father's shadow: The son of the female is the shadow of the male. It is often so, indeed; but I wonder how much of the father's substance is in you!"

Falstaff was joking that perhaps Shadow's mother had committed adultery and so there was little of her husband's substance in her son.

"Do you like him, Sir John?" Justice Shallow asked. "Do you think that he will make a good soldier?"

"Shadow will serve for the summer," Falstaff said. "Prick him, for we have a number of shadows to fill up the muster-book."

"Shadow" was a term for a soldier who was nonexistent but whose name was in the roll. Falstaff had a number of shadows in the roll so that he could collect their pay and keep it.

Shadow stepped back.

"Thomas Wart!" Justice Shallow called.

"Where's he?" Falstaff asked.

Wart stepped forward and said, "Here, sir."

"Is your name Wart?" Falstaff asked.

"Yes, sir."

"You are a very ragged Wart," Falstaff said.

This was true. Wart's clothing consisted of rags pinned together.

"Shall I prick him down, Sir John?" Justice Shallow asked.

"It would be superfluous," Falstaff said, "for his apparel is built upon his back and the whole frame stands upon pins. He is like a building that is held together by pins. He is already being pricked by the pins holding his clothing together, so let us prick him no more."

"Ha, ha, ha!" Justice Shallow said. "You can do it, sir; you can do it. You can make a joke! I commend you well."

Wart stepped back and Justice Shallow called, "Francis Feeble!"

Feeble stepped forward and said, "Here, sir."

"What trade are you in, Feeble?" Falstaff asked.

"I am a woman's tailor, sir."

"Shall I prick him, sir?" Justice Shallow said.

"You may," Falstaff said, "but if he had been a man's tailor, he would have pricked you with one or more of his pins."

He asked Feeble, "Will you make as many holes in an enemy's front line as you have made in a woman's petticoat?"

"I will do my best, sir," Feeble said. "You can have no more than that."

"Well said, good woman's tailor!" Falstaff replied. "Well said, courageous Feeble! You will be as valiant as the wrathful dove or most stout-hearted mouse."

He added, "Prick the woman's tailor well, Master Shallow; prick his name deeply, Master Shallow."

"I wish Wart might have been drafted, sir," Feeble said.

"I wish that you were a man's tailor," Falstaff said, "so that you might mend his clothing and make him fit to go. I cannot draft Wart as a private because he is the leader of so many thousands — of lice. Let that answer be enough for you, most forcible Feeble."

"It shall suffice, sir," Feeble said, stepping back.

"I am bound to you, reverend Feeble," Falstaff said.

He asked Justice Shallow, "Who is next?"

"Peter Bullcalf from the village green!" Justice Shallow called.

"Yes, let's see Bullcalf," Falstaff said.

Bullcalf, who was a strong young man, stepped forward and said, "Here, sir."

"By God, here is a likely fellow!" Falstaff said. "Come, prick Bullcalf until he roars again."

Bull calves were known for bellowing, and when a bull was pricked in a bullfight, it would bellow.

Bullcalf, who did not want to go to war, said, "Oh, Lord! My good Captain —"

"What, are you roaring before you have been pricked?" Falstaff said.

"Oh, Lord, sir! I am a diseased man."

"What disease do you have?" Falstaff asked.

"A very bad cold, sir, a cough, sir, which I caught as I rang the bells to celebrate the anniversary of King Henry IV's coronation day, sir."

"Come, you shall go to the wars in an invalid's gown," Falstaff said. "We will take away your cold with us, and I will leave orders for my friends to ring the bells for you."

Unhappy, Bullcalf stepped back.

Falstaff asked Justice Shallow, "Is this everybody?"

"To give you a choice of the best men, here are two more than the number you must draft," Justice Shallow said. "You must draft four soldiers from here, sir, and you have seen everybody. Therefore, please go in and have dinner with me."

"I will go drink with you," Falstaff said, "but I cannot stay for dinner. I am truly glad to see you, Master Shallow."

"Oh, Sir John, do you remember when we lay all night in the windmill in Saint George's field?" Justice Shallow asked. He was remembering the wild times of his youth again: drinking, staying up all night, and whoring.

"No more of that, good Master Shallow, no more of that," Falstaff said. He still did the things that Justice Shallow had given up decades ago.

"Ha! It was a merry night," Justice Shallow said. "And is Jane Nightwork still alive?"

Since her last name was "Nightwork," no one needs to guess at Jane's occupation.

"She is still alive, Master Shallow."

"She could never stand me."

"Never, never," Falstaff agreed. "She would always say she could not stand Master Shallow."

"By the Mass, I could anger her to the heart," Justice Shallow said. "She was then a fine-looking woman. Does she hold her own well?"

"She is old, old, Master Shallow."

"She must be old now," Justice Shallow said. "She cannot choose but be old; it is certain that she's old. She had her son, Robin Nightwork, by old Nightwork before I came to Clement's Inn."

"That's fifty-five years ago," Justice Silence said.

"Ha, cousin Silence," Justice Shallow said. "I wish that you had seen the things that this knight and I have seen! Ha, Sir John, isn't that the truth!"

"We have heard the chimes at midnight, Master Shallow," Falstaff replied.

"That we have, that we have, that we have," Justice Shallow said. "Truly, Sir John, we have. Our motto was 'Hem, boys! Clear your throat, and down the hatch!' Come, let's go to dinner; come, let's go to dinner. Jesus, the days that we have seen! Come, come."

Falstaff and the two justices departed.

Bullcalf saw a chance to get out of military service. He said, "Good Master Corporate Bardolph, be my friend, and take these four Harry ten shillings in French crowns. They are worth one pound. Truly, sir, I had rather be hanged, sir, than go to war, and yet, for my own part, sir, I do not care; but rather, because I am unwilling, and, for my own part, I have a desire to stay with my friends; else, sir, I did not care, for my own part, so much."

Of course, he cared greatly — he did NOT want to go to war. However, he did not want to confess to cowardice.

"I see," Bardolph said. "Stand over there."

Moldy was especially worried about fighting in the army. He said to Bardolph, "And, good master Corporal Captain, for my old wife's sake, be my friend. She has nobody to do anything about her when I am gone; and she is old, and cannot help herself: You shall have forty shillings, sir. They are worth two pounds."

"I see," Bardolph said. "Stand over there."

Feeble witnessed what was happening. An honorable man, he said, "Truly, I do not wish to avoid my military service through dishonest means. A man can die but once, and we owe God a debt that can be paid only with our death. I will not act dishonorably. If it is my destiny to die in battle, so be it; if it is not my destiny to die in battle, so be it. No man is too good to serve his Prince. So let me die in battle or not die in battle. A man who dies this year owes no death the following year."

"Well said," Bardolph replied. "You are a good man."

This did not mean that Bardolph would not accept the bribes of Bullcalf and Moldy.

"Truly, I will do nothing dishonorable," Feeble declared.

Falstaff and the two justices returned.

"Come, sir, which men shall I have?" Falstaff said.

"Whichever four you want," Justice Shallow replied.

Bardolph said to Falstaff, "Sir, may I have a word with you." He whispered, "I have been offered three pounds not to draft Moldy and Bullcalf."

"I see," Falstaff said. "Good!"

"Come, Sir John, which four will you have?" Justice Shallow said.

"You choose for me," Falstaff said.

Justice Shallow chose the men that most men would agree would make the best soldiers: "Moldy, Bullcalf, Feeble, and Shadow."

"Moldy and Bullcalf!" Falstaff said. "As for you, Moldy, old man, stay at home until you are past service: and as for you, Bullcalf, youngster, grow until you come of age to be of service. I want neither of you."

Falstaff was saying — falsely — that Moldy was too old for military service and that Bullcalf was too young for military service.

"Sir John, Sir John, do not yourself wrong," Justice Shallow objected. "They are the men likeliest to be good soldiers, and I want you to have the best men you can get."

"Will you tell me, Master Shallow, how to choose a man for military service?" Falstaff said. "Care I for the body, the strength, the height, the bulk, and the overall physical bigness of a man! Give me the spirit, Master Shallow.

"Here's Wart; you see what a ragged appearance he has, and yet he shall charge at you and discharge a light musket with the motion of a pewterer's hammer that rapidly taps-taps-taps metal into shape. He will run to the front, fire his weapon, and then run back to reload faster than a man gulps the contents of a brewer's beer bucket.

"And look at this half-faced fellow, Shadow. He is so thin and narrow that you can't even see his face unless he is standing sideways. Give me this man: He presents no target to the enemy. The enemy may as accurately aim at the edge of a penknife. And as for a retreat; how swiftly will this Feeble the woman's tailor run away!

"Oh, give me the spare, thin men, and spare me the great ones.

"Put a light musket into Wart's hand, Bardolph."

Bardolph gave Wart a light musket and then ordered, "March! Hut! Hut! Hut!"

"Come, show me what you can do with your light musket," Falstaff said. "Good. Very good. Go on. Very good. Exceedingly good. Oh, give me always a little, lean, old, dried-up, bald gunman. Well done, truly, Wart; you are a good scab. Wait, here's sixpence for you."

Falstaff gave Wart a coin.

"He has not mastered marching," Justice Shallow said. "He is not marching correctly. I remember at Mile-end Green, when I was staying at Clement's Inn — I was then playing Sir Dagonet, King Arthur's fool, in the exhibition of archery dedicated to Arthur. I remember a nimble little fellow who really knew how to handle a musket. He would do this, and this, and this —"

Justice Shallow demonstrated the various maneuvers.

"— and he would say 'rah, tah, tah,' imitating the loading of the musket, and then he would run in front of the front line, and then he would say 'boom," imitating the discharge of the musket, and he would retreat and then come forward again. I shall never again see such a fellow."

"These fellows I have drafted will also do well, Master Shallow," Falstaff said. "May God keep you well, Master Silence. I will not talk your ear off. Fare you well, both of you gentlemen. I thank you. I must travel a dozen miles tonight."

He then said, "Bardolph, give the soldiers uniforms."

"Sir John, may the Lord bless you!" Justice Shallow said. "May God prosper your affairs! May God send us peace! At your return, visit our house; let our old acquaintance be renewed; perhaps I will go with you to the court."

"I swear to God that I wish you would, Master Shallow," Falstaff said.

"Good," Justice Shallow said. "I was not kidding. May God keep you well."

"Fare you well, gentle gentlemen," Falstaff said.

The two justices departed.

"Forward, Bardolph," Falstaff ordered, "lead the men away."

Everyone left except Falstaff, who said to himself, "When I return, I will take advantage of and cheat these justices. I can see the bottom of Justice Shallow — I can see through him. Lord, Lord, how susceptible we old men are to this vice of lying! This same starved, skinny justice has done nothing but prate to me about the wildness of his youth, and the feats he once did about Turnbull Street, a favorite gathering place for thieves and whores, and every third word he has spoken is a lie that he pays to the hearer quicker than a Turk pays tribute to the Sultan — who punished those who paid tribute late by killing them.

"I remember Shallow when he was at Clement's Inn. He looked like a man who had been carved from a piece of cheese left after supper. When he was naked, he was, for all the world, like a forked radish, with a head fantastically carved upon it with a knife. He was so skinny and wretched that his dimensions to any imperfect sight were invincible: He would have been good in a battle because no one with less than perfect sight could see and shoot him — to an enemy soldier with bad eyesight, he would be invisible. He was the very embodiment of famine; yet he was as lecherous as a monkey, and the whores called him a mandrake because it is supposed to be an aphrodisiac.

"He always adopted fashionable things just after they went out of fashion, and he sang tunes to the worn-out whores that he had heard the wagon drivers whistle, and he would swear that they were his own fanciful musical compositions and serenades. And now this Vice's dagger — this skinny piece of wood — has become a squire, and talks as familiarly of John of Gaunt as if he had been sworn brother to him; and I'll be sworn that he never saw John of Gaunt except once at a jousting tournament, where John of Gaunt hit him on the head for crowding among the Marshal's men. I saw it, and I told John of Gaunt that he had beaten his own name because you could have thrust Shallow and all his apparel into a long, skinny eel-skin. The case for a long, skinny treble oboe — the smallest oboe — was a mansion for Justice Shallow, it was an entire court, and now he owns land and cattle. Well, I will seek his company, if I return, and I won't forgive myself if I don't make him a philosopher's two stones to me. I intend to make him a source of profit for myself — as profitable as if I had the philosopher's stone that will turn base metal into gold and the philosopher's stone — or *elixir vitae*, aka elixir of life — that will keep a man forever young.

"If a young and small fish can be a bait — a temptation and a food — for the old pike, I see no reason in the law of nature why I may not snap at him. The great fish eat the small. Time will tell, and I have nothing more to say."

# CHAPTER 4

## — 4.1 —

At the rebel camp in Gaultree Forest in Yorkshire, the Archbishop of York, Mowbray, Lord Hastings, and others were meeting in an open area.

The Archbishop of York asked, "What is this forest called?"

Hastings replied, "It is Gaultree Forest, if it shall please your grace."

"Let us stand here, my lords," the Archbishop of York said, "and send out scouts to learn the numbers of our enemies."

"We have sent them out already," Hastings said.

"That is well done," the Archbishop of York said. "My friends and brethren in these great affairs, I must tell you that I have received letters recently from Northumberland. This is their cold intent, tenor, and substance: He says that he wishes that he could be here with such an army as someone of his rank and position ought to have, but he could not raise such an army, and therefore he has gone to Scotland to increase his power, and he concludes with hearty prayers that you and your armies may survive the hazard and fearful meeting of the armies that oppose them."

"Thus do the hopes we have in him touch bottom like a ship and dash themselves to pieces," Hastings said. "We will receive no reinforcements from Northumberland."

A messenger arrived and Hastings asked, "What news do you bring?"

"West of this forest, scarcely a mile away, in well-ordered formation marches the enemy," the messenger said. "And, by the ground they hide, I judge their number to be approximately thirty thousand."

"That is exactly the number of opposing soldiers that we thought the opposing army would have," Mowbray said. "Let us move on and face them in the field."

Seeing someone from the enemy approaching, the Archbishop of York asked, "Who is the leader in full military regalia coming toward us?"

Mowbray replied, "I think it is the Lord of Westmoreland."

Westmoreland rode up to them and said, "Health and fair greetings from our general: Prince John."

"Speak in peace, Lord of Westmoreland," the Archbishop of York said. "What do you have to say to us?"

"My lord," Westmoreland replied, "I chiefly address my speech to you. If rebellion came like it truly is, in base and abject routs, led on by bloody youth, trimmed with rags, and escorted by Rage, and approved by boys and beggars — I say, if damned rebellion were to so appear in its true, native, and most proper shape, you, reverend father, and these noble lords would not be here to dress the ugly form of base and bloody insurrection with your fair honors. You are lending dignity to undignified rebellion. You, Lord Archbishop, whose diocese is maintained by a civil peace, whose silver beard the hand of peace has touched, whose learning and good letters have been tutored by peace, whose white robes symbolize innocence, the dove and very blessed spirit of peace, why do you so badly translate yourself out of the speech of peace that bears such grace, transforming it to the harsh and boisterous tongue of war? Why are you transforming your books into graves, your ink into blood, your pens into lances, and your divine tongue into a trumpet and call to war?"

"Why do I do this?" the Archbishop of York said. "That is your question to me. Briefly, this is the answer: We are all diseased, and with our gluttonous and overindulgent and wanton hours we have brought ourselves into a burning fever, and we must bleed because of it. Our late sovereign, King Richard II, being infected with this disease, died.

"But, my most noble Lord of Westmoreland, I do not take on me here the role of a physician who makes men bleed, or do I as an enemy to peace troop here in the throngs of military men. Instead, I am making a show of fearful war in order to cure minds that are sick because of overindulgence and in order to purge the obstructions that begin to stop our very veins of life.

"Hear me more plainly. I have in equal and unbiased balance justly weighed what wrongs our arms may do against what wrongs we suffer, and I have found that our griefs are heavier than our offences. The rough torrent of occasion and the present rough circumstances have forced us away from the quiet we enjoyed. We have the summary of all our griefs written down so that we can reveal them at the proper time. Long ago, we offered this document to King Henry IV, but we were not allowed to see him and give him the document. We are denied access to the King by those men who have most done us wrong.

"The dangers of the days but newly gone, whose memory is written on the earth with still visible blood, and the bad events that happen every minute now, have made us put on this seemingly unbefitting armor.

"We do not wish to disrupt the peace or any part of it; instead, we wish to establish here a peace — one that is worthy of the name."

Westmoreland replied, "When has your appeal ever been denied? How have you been oppressed by the King? What lord has been ordered to harm you? What has been done to you that you should seal this lawless bloody book of forged rebellion with a divine seal and consecrate the bitter edge of rebellion?"

"I am here with the rebellion because of my brothers general and my brother born. My brothers general are the citizens in this commonwealth who suffer. They are my brothers because they are my fellow citizens. King Henry IV had my birth brother, Lord Scroop, executed, and that is my personal and particular reason for being involved with this rebellion. My brother died without even being allowed to receive the final sacrament."

"There is no need of any such redress — reparation and compensation — as you are demanding," Westmoreland said, "and if there were, the redress would not go to you."

Mowbray replied, "Why shouldn't the redress go to him in part because of the murder of his brother, and to us all who feel the bruises of these days and suffer the condition of these times that lay a heavy and unequal hand upon our honors? We have suffered wrongs."

"My good Lord Mowbray," Westmoreland said, "this is a time of war, and some things are necessary to do in times of war. Consider the times, and you shall say indeed that it is the times, and not the King, that are doing you injuries.

"Yet for your part, it does not appear to me that you have any inch of any ground — any reason — on which to build a grief against either King Henry IV or the times," Westmoreland said. "The estates of your father, the noble and very well remembered Duke of Norfolk, were taken from him, but haven't they been restored to you?"

Thomas Mowbray, the Duke of Norfolk, was a rival of Henry Bolingbrook, now King Henry IV. King Richard II had banished Thomas Mowbray, the

Duke of Norfolk. His son was also named Thomas Mowbray — he was the Thomas Mowbray who now was speaking.

Mowbray replied, "What thing, in honor, had my father lost that now needs to be revived and animated in me? King Richard II respected him, but because of circumstances was forced to banish him.

"At Coventry, Harry Bolingbroke and my father intended to fight a duel. They had mounted their horses and were eager to face each other. Their neighing coursers waited excitedly for the spurs that would order them to charge. The beavers of the dueling men's helmets were down. Their eyes of fire sparked through sights of steel, and the loud trumpet blew that it was time for them to charge each other. Then, then, when there was nothing that could have stopped my father from attacking the breast of Bolingbroke, King Richard II threw down his staff of command and stopped the duel. His own life hung upon the staff he threw down. When he threw down his staff of command, at the same time he threw down his own life and all the lives of those who have died because of Bolingbroke's indictments and wars. If the duel had been allowed to continue, my father would have killed Bolingbroke and there would be no King Henry IV."

"Lord Mowbray, you don't know what you are saying," Westmoreland said. "Bolingbroke was then reputed to be the most valiant gentleman in England. Who knows on whom fortune would then have smiled? Who knows who would have won the duel? But if your father had been victor there, he would never have made it alive out of Coventry because everyone there hated him, and they gave all their prayers and love to Bolingbrook, whom they loved and blessed and graced more than they did King Richard II.

"But this is mere digression from my purpose in coming here. I have come here from Prince John, our general, to learn your grievances and to tell you from his grace that he will give you audience; and if it should appear that your demands are just, they shall be met. Of course, he will not agree to any demands that make him think that you are enemies of the King."

"But he has forced us to compel him to make this offer to us," Mowbray said. "And he is making this offer from political considerations, not from any respect for us. This is a cold, calculated political maneuver."

"Mowbray, you are presumptuous to think that," Westmoreland said. "This offer comes from mercy, not from fear. Look! Our army is within our sight.

Upon my honor, I swear that our army is much too confident to give a single thought to fear. Our army has many more men of military renown than yours, our men are better trained in the use of arms, our armor is at least as strong, our cause is the best. You should be thinking that we are making this offer because our heart is good, not because we are forced to make it."

"Well, I say we shall admit no parley," Mowbray said. "We will not have a conference with Prince John of Lancaster."

"That is evidence that you are in the wrong," Westmoreland said. "A rotten case abides no handling. A rotten container falls apart when it is touched, and a rotten cause falls apart when it is examined."

Hastings asked, "Has Prince John full authority, as a plenipotentiary of his father, King Henry IV, to listen to our grievances and to come to a legal agreement with us?"

"Obviously, he does," Westmoreland said. "The King made the Prince the general of this army. I am surprised that you would ask such a question."

The Archbishop of York said, "Then take, my Lord of Westmoreland, this document; it contains a list of our general grievances. If each of the several different grievances herein is redressed, and if all the members of our rebellion, both here and elsewhere, that strengthen and form a part of our rebellion, are given a true and substantial and legal pardon and immediate satisfaction of our requests, we will again return to our boundaries and will return to peace. We will no longer be like a flooding river but will instead return to within the peaceful banks of the river."

"I will show Prince John, our general, this document," Westmoreland said. "If you agree, lords, we can meet in the middle of the no-man's-land in between our armies. Within sight of our armies, we can either make an agreement that ends in peace, if God is willing, or we can make an agreement to do battle against each other."

"My lord, we will meet Prince John," the Archbishop of York said.

Westmoreland departed, carrying the document.

Mowbray said, "I have a feeling in my heart that no conditions of our peace can stand. Even if we agree to a peace, there will be no peace."

"Don't think that," Hastings said. "If we can make our peace with such large and absolute terms as we shall insist on, then our peace shall stand on ground as firm as rocky mountains."

"Yes, but the King shall be suspicious of us. He will regard us in such a way that every supposed slight and every false accusation and every idle, petty, and frivolous fault shall remind the King of this rebellion. Even if we were as devoted to the King as martyrs, we shall be winnowed with so rough a wind that even our corn shall seem as light as chaff. He will hold us to a standard that no one can attain, and he will not see the good things that we will do. He will see only bad even when we do good."

"No, no, my lord," the Archbishop of York said. "Note this: The King is weary of dainty and trifling grievances. He has learned that to end one danger by killing the offender results in reviving two greater dangers among those who are still alive. Killing one supposed enemy results in the creation of two real enemies. Therefore, King Henry IV will wipe the tablet clean and will forget anything that would bring to mind what has happened here. He knows very well that he cannot weed this land of just anyone whom he suspects of being an enemy. His foes are so enrooted with his friends that, when he plucks an enemy to remove him, he ends up hurting a friend. He is in the situation of a husband who has been so enraged that he wants to strike his wife. He raises his arm so that he can hit her, but she hold his infant up, and he stops his arm before it lashes out at her."

"Besides," Hastings said, "King Henry IV has wasted all his rods on recent offenders, and he now lacks the instruments of chastisement. He is like a fangless lion: He can threaten to hurt someone, but he cannot hurt anyone."

"That is very true," the Archbishop of York said. "And therefore be assured, my good Lord Marshal Mowbray, if we do now well make our atonement, our peace will be like a broken bone that has mended. It has grown stronger after being broken."

"I hope that you are right," Mowbray said. "I see that Westmoreland is returning now."

Westmoreland arrived and said, "Prince John is near. Does it please you to meet him at an equal distance between our armies? Does it please you to meet him in no-man's-land? If it does, Archbishop of York, move forward."

"Go ahead of us and greet Prince John," the Archbishop of York said. "Tell him that we are coming to meet him."

In no-man's-land, at an equal distance between the two armies, the two opposing sides met. On one side were the Archbishop of York, Hastings, Mowbray, and others; on the other side were Prince John of Lancaster, Westmoreland, and others.

"It is good to see you, Mowbray," Prince John of Lancaster said. "Good day to you, gentle Archbishop of York, and also to you, Lord Hastings, and to all.

"My Lord Archbishop of York, you acted better and more honorably when your flock, assembled after hearing the church bell, encircled you to hear with reverence your exposition on the holy text: the Bible. You acted better then than you do now. You are now an iron man. You are encased in armor, and you are cheering a rout of rebels with the drum of your words. You are turning the word to sword and turning life to death.

"That man who sits within a monarch's heart, and ripens in the sunshine of the King's favor, why would he abuse the support of the King? What mischiefs might he open and set abroad in the shadow of such greatness!

"You, Archbishop of York, are doing that. Who has not heard it spoken how deeply learned you were within the books of God and how much you were in God's favor? To us you were the Speaker in God's celestial Parliament; we imagined that you spoke for God himself! To us you were the interpreter of God's grace and the sanctities of Heaven, and you were the messenger who brought a Godly perspective to our dull imaginings.

"Who shall believe anything other than that you misuse the reverence of your position as Archbishop and employ the appearance of Heavenly favor as you do dishonorable deeds, the way that a false and traitorous favorite misuses his Prince's name as he does dishonorable deeds?

"Under the counterfeited zeal of God, you have taken up the subjects of his deputy, my father, King Henry IV; against both the peace of Heaven and the peace of my father's Kingdom, you have made his subjects swarm up like angry bees in rebellion. You profess a false zeal for God, and you pretend that you are acting with God's approval and seal."

"My good Prince John of Lancaster, I am not here against your father's peace," the Archbishop of York said, "but, as I told Westmoreland, the mistempered times do, as everyone knows, crowd us and crush us and force us to do this abnormal act of rebellion in order to protect our safety.

"I sent your grace a document listing the detailed particulars of our grievances, a document that previously has been with scorn shoved from the court. As a result of that scornful action, this Hydra — this many-headed — son of war is born, whose dangerous eyes may well be charmed asleep if the King grants us our most just and right desires. If he does that, this mad rebellion will be cured, and his truly obedient subjects will once more bow tamely at the foot of his majesty."

"If these wrongs are not righted," Mowbray said, "we are ready to try our fortunes in battle to the last man."

"And even if we here fall down," Hastings said, "we have reinforcements to second our attempt. If they miscarry, their reinforcements shall second them. And so generation after generation of rebels shall be born, and heir from heir shall continue this rebellion as long as generations are born in England."

"You are too shallow, Hastings, much too shallow, to sound the bottom of the after-times," Prince John of Lancaster said. "You are unable to peer very far into the future."

"Does it please your grace to answer these men directly," Westmoreland asked, "and tell them whether you will make right their grievances?"

"I have read the articles in their document, and I will make right all their grievances," Prince John of Lancaster said. "I swear here and now, by the honor of my blood, that my father's purposes and actions have been misunderstood, and some of the people acting under his orders have misinterpreted his meaning and misused their authority.

"Archbishop of York, these grievances shall quickly be redressed — upon my soul, they shall. If this may please you, discharge your soldiers and allow them to return to their different counties, and we will do the same thing. Here in between the two opposing armies let us drink together as friend and embrace each other, so that all their eyes may carry home those tokens of our restored respect and amity."

"I take your Princely word for these redresses," the Archbishop of York said.

"I give it to you, and I will maintain my word," Prince John of Lancaster said, "and now I will drink to your grace."

Hastings said, "Go, Captain, and deliver to the rebel army this news of peace. Let them have their pay, and let them depart. I know it will well please them. Hurry, Captain."

The Captain left to carry out his orders.

The Archbishop of York made a toast: "To you, my noble Lord of Westmoreland."

"I pledge your grace," Westmoreland replied, "and, if you knew what pains I have taken to breed this present peace, you would drink freely. But my respect for you shall show itself more openly hereafter."

"I do not doubt you," the Archbishop of York replied.

"I am glad to hear it," Westmoreland replied.

Westmoreland proposed a toast: "Health to Mowbray."

"You wish me health at a very good time," Mowbray said, "for suddenly I feel ill."

"When evil is coming, men are always merry," the Archbishop of York said. "When men feel sad, it is a harbinger of good things."

"Therefore be merry, Archbishop," Westmoreland said, "since sudden sorrow serves to say this: 'Some good thing will happen tomorrow.'"

"Believe me, I am very light in spirit," the Archbishop of York said.

"That is a bad thing," Mowbray said, "if you were right when you said, 'When evil is coming, men are always merry.'"

They heard some shouting.

"The news of peace has been given to the soldiers," Prince John of Lancaster said. "Listen to how they shout!"

"This noise would have been cheerful after a victory," Mowbray said.

"A peace is of the nature of a conquest and a victory," the Archbishop of York said. "For then both parties are nobly subdued, and neither party is the loser."

"Go, my lord," Prince John of Lancaster said, "and let our army be discharged, too."

Westmoreland departed.

Prince John of Lancaster said to the Archbishop of York, "And, my good lord, if it pleases you, let our armies march by us so that we may see the men who would have fought each other in battle."

The Archbishop of York said, "Go, good Lord Hastings, and, before they are dismissed, let them march by us."

Hastings departed.

Prince John of Lancaster said, "I hope, lords, that we shall stay together in the same camp tonight."

Westmoreland came back.

Prince John of Lancaster asked him, "Why is our army still here?"

"The leaders, because they have orders from you to stay here, will not leave until you personally order them to leave."

"They know their orders and their duty," Prince John of Lancaster said.

Hastings returned and said to the Archbishop of York, "My lord, our army has been dispersed. Like youthful steers who have been unyoked, they take their courses East, West, North, South. They are like students leaving school; each hurries toward his home and playground."

"That is good news, my Lord Hastings," Westmoreland said. "I now arrest you, traitor, for high treason. I also arrest you, Archbishop of York, and you, Lord Mowbray. I arrest both of you for high treason, which is punishable by death."

"Is this proceeding just and honorable?" Mowbray asked.

"Is your rebellion just and honorable?" Westmoreland replied.

"Will you thus break your faith?" the Archbishop of York said to Prince John of Lancaster.

"I did not promise you a pardon," Prince John of Lancaster said. "I promised you redress of these grievances that you complained about, and, by my honor, I will perform that redress with a most Christian care.

"But as for you, rebels, look to taste what is due to rebellion and such acts as yours.

"Most shallowly did you begin this rebellion. You foolishly brought your soldiers, and you foolishly sent them home."

He ordered, "Strike up our drums, and pursue the scattered stragglers among the rebels. God, and not we, has safely fought today.

"Someone guard these traitors and take them to the block of death, which is treason's true bed and yielder up of breath. There they shall be beheaded."

Prince John of Lancaster's soldiers were pursuing the rebels and killing or capturing as many of them as they could. Falstaff was one of the soldiers doing the pursuing.

Falstaff saw a rebel and asked, "What's your name, sir? Please tell me your rank, and where you are from."

"I am a knight, sir, and my name is Colevile of the Dale."

A dale is a low, deep place — a valley.

"Well, then, Colevile is your name, a knight is your rank, and your place is the dale," Falstaff said. "Colevile shall still be your name, a traitor will be your rank, and your place will be in a dungeon. That is a low, deep place, and so you shall still be Colevile of the Dale."

"Aren't you Sir John Falstaff?" Colevile asked.

"I am as good a man as he, sir, whoever I am," Falstaff replied. "Do you surrender, sir? Or shall I sweat as I fight you? If I sweat, my drops of sweat will be the drops that fall from the eyes of your friends as they mourn your death; therefore, rouse your fear and trembling, and do homage to me by kneeling before me."

Colevile knelt and said, "I think that you are Sir John Falstaff, and therefore I surrender."

Sir John Falstaff was thought to have killed Hotspur at Shrewsbury, and that had given him an undeserved reputation as a mighty warrior.

"I have a whole school — a large number — of tongues in this belly of mine," Falstaff said, "and not a tongue of them all speaks any other word but my name. People look at my huge belly and immediately know my identity. If I had a belly of normal size, I would be the most energetic — but anonymous — fellow in Europe. My womb, my womb, my womb — my belly — undoes me."

He looked up and said, "Here comes our general."

Prince John of Lancaster, Westmoreland, and Sir John Blunt came over to Falstaff and Colevile.

Prince John of Lancaster said, "The time for urgency of action is past; let us no longer pursue the rebels. Call back our soldiers, good Westmoreland."

Westmoreland left to carry out this order.

Prince John of Lancaster said, "Now, Falstaff, where have you been all this while? When everything is over and done, then you show up. These tardy tricks of yours will, I swear by my life, result in your sometime or other breaking some gallows' back. You will be hung, and because you are so heavy, you will break the gallows."

"I am sorry, my lord, that you should think that way," Falstaff said. "I have never known yet when rebuke and threat were not the reward of valor. Do you think that I am a swallow, an arrow, or a bullet? Do you think that I can travel as quickly as a swallow, an arrow, or a bullet? Do I have, in my poor and old motion, the ability to cover ground as quickly as thought? I have speeded hither with the very quickest speed possible; I have exhausted more than one hundred and eighty horses traveling here from post to post, and here, stained by travel as I am, I have with my pure and immaculate valor captured Sir John Colevile of the Dale, a most furious knight and valorous enemy. Isn't that worthy of praise? He saw me, and he yielded. I may justly say, with the hook-nosed fellow of Rome, Julius Caesar, that 'I came, saw, and overcame.'"

"Your capturing him was more his doing than your own," Prince John of Lancaster said. He thought, *Sir John Colevile of the Dale surrendered to you instead of fighting you.*

"I don't know about that," Falstaff said. "Here he is, and here I give him to you, and I beg your grace, let this be recorded with the rest of this day's notable deeds. By the Lord, if it is not, I will have printed a ballad about my valor, with my own picture on the top of it, showing Colevile kissing my foot. If I am forced to do that, and if you do not all look like gilded counterfeits compared to me, and if I in the clear sky of fame do not outshine you as much as the full Moon outshines the cinders of the element, aka the stars in the sky, which appear to be like the shiny heads of pins compared to the Moon, then do not believe the word of noble men. Therefore, let me have the credit that is rightfully mine, and let my just rewards mount high."

"Yours is too heavy to mount," Prince John of Lancaster said. He meant that Falstaff's belly was too heavy for him to ascend or climb high.

"Let it shine, then," Falstaff replied.

"Yours is too thick to shine," Prince John of Lancaster said. He meant that Falstaff's belly was too thick for light to shine through. Thick can also mean dense, and Prince John of Lancaster, who did not like Falstaff, was saying — falsely — that Falstaff's intellect was too dense for his wit to shine.

"Let it do something, my good lord, that may do me good, and call it what you will," Falstaff said.

Prince John of Lancaster asked the prisoner, "Is your name Colevile?"

"It is, my lord."

"You are a famous rebel, Colevile."

"And a famous and true subject took him," Falstaff said.

"I am, my lord, like my superiors are who led me here," Colevile said. "If they had been ruled by me and I had been their leader, you would not have won the day so easily. This victory would have cost you."

"I do not know how your fellow rebels sold themselves," Falstaff said, "but you, like a kind fellow, gave yourself away gratis — free — and I thank you for it."

Westmoreland returned.

Prince John of Lancaster asked him, "Now, have you ordered that the pursuit of the rebels cease?"

"Our soldiers have retreated, and they have stopped pursuing the rebels."

"We will send Colevile with his confederates to York for immediate execution," Prince John of Lancaster said. "Blunt, lead him hence; and see that you guard him well."

He added, "And now we will hurry home to the court, my lords. I hear that the King my father is very sick. Our good news shall go before us to his majesty."

He said to Westmoreland, "You shall bear this good news to comfort my father, and we with sober and temperate speed will follow you."

"My lord Prince John of Lancaster, please give me permission to go home through Gloucestershire," Falstaff requested, "and, when you arrive at your father's court, speak well of me in your report."

"Fare you well, Falstaff," Prince John said. "I, as Prince, shall speak better of you than you deserve."

Everyone departed except Falstaff, who said to himself, "I wish that you had wit, Prince John of Lancaster. Wit is worth more than your Dukedom. Truly, this young sober-blooded boy does not like me, and no man can make him laugh, but that's no marvel — he never drinks wine.

"None of these demure boys ever come to any good because weak beer, which very thoroughly cools their blood, and the many meals they make of fish cause them to fall into a kind of male green-sickness — the anemia that is usually suffered by young girls — and then when they marry, they give birth to girls, not boys. They are generally fools and cowards. Some of us would be fools and cowards, too, except for the inflammation wrought by intoxication.

"A good sherry wine has a two-fold effect on its drinker. The first effect of your excellent sherry wine is that it ascends into the brain and gets rid of all the foolish and dull and curdled thoughts that inhabit it. Wine makes the brain quick in understanding, full of nimble fiery and delectable thoughts, which, delivered over to the tongue, which gives birth to the voice, becomes excellent wit.

"The second effect of your excellent sherry wine is the warming of the blood. Before intoxication, the blood is cold and settled, white and pale — the badge of pusillanimity and cowardice. But the sherry wine warms the blood and makes it move from the insides to the outermost parts. It brightens the face, which like a beacon gives warning to all the rest of this little Kingdom, man, to take up weapons and be ready to fight. The vital and not-so-vital spirits report to their Captain, the heart, which, great and puffed up with this retinue, does any deed of courage, and this valor and courage comes from sherry wine. Skill in the handling of weapons is nothing without wine because wine puts that knowledge of weapons to work. Learning by itself is like a hoard of gold guarded by a Devil — the gold cannot be used. But sherry wine sets the learning free and allows it to be used in action. The learning graduates and ceases to be theoretical knowledge and instead becomes practical knowledge.

"That is why Prince Hal is valiant. He naturally inherited cold blood from his father, but he has cultivated his cold blood, like one would cultivate lean, sterile, and bare land. He has manured, aka fertilized, husbanded, and tilled his cold blood with the excellent endeavor of drinking well a good quantity of fertile sherry wine, and by so doing, he has become very hot and valiant.

"If I had a thousand sons, the first human and secular principle I would teach them would be to never drink weak beer and to instead addict themselves to sherry wine."

Say what you will about Falstaff, his opinions were often interesting and contrary to conventional thinking.

Bardolph walked over to Falstaff, who asked him, "What is the news?"

Bardolph replied, "The army has been discharged, and all of the soldiers are gone."

"Let them go," Falstaff said. "I'll travel home by way of Gloucestershire; there I will visit Master Robert Shallow, esquire. I have him already softening like wax between my finger and my thumb, and shortly I will seal with him some kind of agreement that will be advantageous to me.

"Let's go."

In the Jerusalem Chamber in the palace at Westminster, King Henry IV was meeting with two of his sons: Prince Thomas of Clarence and Prince Humphrey of Gloucester. Warwick and others were also present.

Using the royal plural, King Henry IV said, "Now, lords, if God gives a successful end to this civil war that bleeds at our doors, we will lead our youthful soldiers on to higher fields and draw no swords but those that will be sanctified in a Holy Crusade.

"Our navy is ready, our army has been collected, our deputies who will rule England in my absence have been well selected, and everything lies in accordance to our wish. However, we are lacking a little personal strength, and we must pause until these rebels, which are now afoot, come underneath the yoke of government."

Warwick said, "We doubt not but your majesty shall soon enjoy the revival of your strength and the defeat of the rebels."

"Humphrey, my son of Gloucester," Henry IV said, "where is Prince Hal, your brother?"

Prince Humphrey of Gloucester replied, "I think he has gone to hunt, my lord, at Windsor."

"And who is accompanying him?"

"I do not know, my lord."

"Isn't his brother, Prince Thomas of Clarence, with him?"

"No, my good lord; Prince Thomas of Clarence is here."

Prince Thomas of Clarence asked, "What does my lord and father want?"

"Nothing but good to you, Prince Thomas of Clarence," Henry IV said. "How does it happen that you are not with Prince Hal, your brother? He loves you, and you are neglecting him, Thomas. You have a better place in his affection than all your brothers. He likes you better than his other brothers. Cherish this, my boy, and you may be able to do noble deeds of mediation, after I am dead, between his greatness — he will be King Henry V then — and your other brothers.

"Therefore, do not neglect him; do not do anything to blunt his love for you, nor lose the good advantage of his grace by seeming cold or careless of his will. Prince Hal is gracious, if he is respected. He has a tear with which to show pity, and he has a hand as open as day for giving charity. However, when he is incensed and angry, he is like flint, as changeable as winter and as sudden as icy squalls at dawn. His temper, therefore, must be well observed: Chide him for faults, and do it reverently, when you perceive his blood inclined to mirth. But if he is moody, give him time and scope, until his passions, like a whale grounded on a beach, exhausts and kills itself by struggling to return to the sea. Learn this, Thomas, and you shall prove to be a shelter to your friends. You will be a hoop of gold to link and bind your brothers, so that the united vessel of their blood, even when confronted by the poisonous venom of rumor and criticism, as, no doubt, will happen, shall never be harmed, though the forces against their union are as strong as poisonous wolf's bane or rash and impetuous gunpowder."

"I shall watch out for him with all my care and love," Prince Thomas of Clarence said.

"Why aren't you at Windsor with him, Prince Thomas of Clarence?"

"He is not there today," Prince Thomas of Clarence said. "He dines in London."

"And who are his companions? Can you tell me that?"

"He is with Poins, and all his other usual companions."

"Weeds grow best in the richest soil," Henry IV said. "Prince Hal, the noble image of my youth, is run over with them; therefore, my grief stretches itself beyond the hour of my death. The blood weeps from my heart when I imagine the days of misrule and rotten times that you shall look upon when I am dead and sleeping with my ancestors. For when Prince Hal's headstrong riot has no curb, when rage and hot blood are his counselors, when means and opportunity and licentious manners meet together, with what wings shall his natural propensities fly towards the danger and downfall confronting him!"

"My gracious lord," Warwick said, "you misunderstand him. Prince Hal is studying his base companions the way he would study a foreign language. To learn the language, it is necessary for him to look upon and learn even the most immodest words. Once he has learned those immodest words, he will then use them no further but will instead hate them. I hope that your highness realizes that Prince Hal will eventually cast off his gross companions the way that students cast off gross words. Their memory shall live on as a pattern or a measure by which he will judge the lives of others. By so doing, he will turn past evils to advantages."

"Seldom do bees leave dead carrion that contains their honeycombs," King Henry IV said. "Bees will sometimes make a hive and store honey in the carcass of a wild beast. Once they do that, they will seldom leave the honey. Prince Hal has found sweetness in the companionship of lowlifes, and it is unlikely that he will leave that sweetness when he becomes King."

Westmoreland entered the room with news from Prince John of Lancaster.

King Henry IV asked, "Who is here? Westmoreland?"

"Health to my sovereign, and may new happiness be added to the good news that I am able to deliver to you!" Westmoreland said. "Your son Prince John kisses your grace's hand. Mowbray, the Archbishop of York, Hastings, and all the other rebels are brought to the punishment of your law. There is not now a rebel's sword unsheathed: Peace puts forth her olive branch everywhere. How this has happened is recounted in detail in this letter, which you may read at your leisure, your highness."

"Oh, Westmoreland, you are a summer bird, which always at the latter end of winter sings to celebrate the increasing hours of daylight."

Harcourt entered the room.

King Henry IV saw him and said, "Look, here's more news."

Harcourt said, "May Heaven keep your majesty safe from your enemies, and when they rise against you, may they fall as have those about whom I have come to tell you news! The Earl of Northumberland and the Lord Bardolph, who had a great army of English and of Scots, have been overthrown by the Sheriff of Yorkshire. You can read about the manner and true order of the battle in this letter, if you wish."

"Why should such good news make me sick?" Henry IV said. "Will fortune never come with both hands full? Instead, she writes her fair words always in the foulest letters! Good never comes only with good, for always some evil is mixed with it. Fortune either gives a person an appetite and no food; such is the case with the poor, who are healthy. Or else Fortune gives a person a feast but takes away their appetite; such is the case with the rich, who have abundance but do not enjoy it. I should rejoice now at this happy news; but instead my eyesight is now failing, and my brain is cloudy. Come here and help me! I am very ill!"

"Take care, your majesty!" Prince Humphrey of Gloucester said.

"Oh, my royal father!" Prince Thomas of Clarence said.

"My sovereign lord, cheer yourself up, look up," Westmoreland said.

The King fainted.

"Be patient, Princes," Warwick said. "You know that these fits are very common with his highness. Stand back and away from him. Give him air; he'll soon be well."

"No, no, he cannot long hold out against these pangs of pain and illness," Prince Thomas of Clarence said. "The incessant care and labor of his mind has worn the wall — the body — that should contain his life so thin that life looks through and will break out of his body."

"The people frighten me," Prince Humphrey of Gloucester said, "for they observe unfathered heirs and loathsome births of nature. They have witnessed children whose fathers are supernatural beings, and they have witnessed monstrous births of nature. The seasons have changed their characters; it is as if the year had found some months asleep and leaped over them."

"The Thames River has thrice flooded with no ebb in between floods," Clarence said, "and the old folk, time's doting chronicles, say the Thames did so a little time before our great-grandfather King Edward III grew ill and died."

"Speak lower, Princes," Warwick said, "because the King is recovering."

"This apoplexy will certainly be his end — his death," Prince Humphrey of Gloucester whispered.

King Henry IV regained consciousness and said, "Please, lift me up, and carry me away from here into some other room. Do it quietly, please."

King Henry IV lay in a bed in another room. With him were his sons Prince Thomas of Clarence and Prince Humphrey of Gloucester. Also with him were Warwick and some others.

"Let there be no noise made, my gentle friends," King Henry IV said, "unless some kindly hand will whisper sleep-inducing music to my weary spirit. Let soft music play."

"Call the musicians in the other room to come here," Warwick said.

"Set my crown upon my pillow here," Henry IV said.

"His eye is hollow, and his color is changing," Prince Thomas of Clarence whispered. "He is growing pale."

"Less noise, less noise!" Warwick said.

Prince Hal entered the far side of the room and asked, "Has anyone seen Prince Thomas of Clarence?"

Prince Thomas replied, "I am here, brother, and I am full of heaviness and sorrow."

"What!" Prince Hal said. "Rain within doors, and none abroad! Your tears are raindrops that fall inside this palace. How is the King?"

"Exceedingly ill," Prince Humphrey of Gloucester said.

"Has he heard the good news yet?" Prince Hal asked. "Tell it to him."

"He altered much upon hearing it," Prince Humphrey of Gloucester said. "Although it was good news, he fell ill."

"If he is sick with joy, he'll recover without medical attention," Prince Hal said.

"Don't make so much noise, my lords," Warwick said. "Sweet Prince, speak low and softly. The King your father wants to sleep."

"Let us withdraw into the other room," Prince Thomas of Clarence said.

Warwick asked Prince Hal, "Will it please your grace to go along with us?"

"No; I will sit and watch here by the King," Prince Hal said.

Everyone departed, leaving Prince Hal alone with his father.

Prince Hal said to himself, "Why does the crown lie there upon my father's pillow? The crown is so troublesome a bedfellow! Oh, polished perturbation! Oh, golden care! You keep the ports of slumber — the eyes — open wide throughout many a watchful night! Father, you are sleeping with the crown now, yet you do not sleep as soundly or half as deeply sweet as he whose head is covered with a homely nightcap as he snores throughout the watch of night. Oh, majesty! When you pinch your bearer, you sit like expensive armor worn in the heat of day; the armor grows hot and scalds the wearer as it keeps the wearer safe.

"By my father's gates of breath — his lips and nose — there lies a downy feather that does not move. If my father were breathing, that light and weightless downy feather must necessarily move. My gracious lord! My father! This sleep is sound indeed; this is a sleep that has divorced and separated so many English Kings from this golden ring the crown.

"Your due from me is tears and heavy sorrows, and my nature, love, and filial tenderness shall, dear father, pay them plenteously to you.

"My due from you is this imperial crown, which as your first-born son and heir, I inherit."

He put the crown on his head and said, "Lo, here it sits, and God shall guard it. Even if the world's whole strength were gathered into one giant arm, that giant arm would not be able to take this inherited honor from me. You left this crown to me, and I will leave it to my son."

Wearing the crown, Prince Hal went into another room.

King Henry IV was not dead yet; he had been breathing shallowly.

He woke up and called, "Warwick! Prince Humphrey of Gloucester! Prince Thomas of Clarence!"

The three men and others hurried into the room.

"Does the King call us?" Prince Thomas of Clarence asked.

"What does your majesty want?" Warwick asked. "How is your grace?"

"Why did you leave me here alone, my lords?" King Henry IV asked them.

"We left my brother Prince Hal here, my liege," Prince Thomas of Clarence said. "He wanted to sit and watch by you."

"The Prince of Wales!" Henry IV said. "Where is he? Let me see him. He is not here."

"This door is open," Warwick said. "He has gone this way."

"He did not pass through the chamber where we stayed," Prince Humphrey of Gloucester said.

"Where is the crown? Who took it from my pillow?"

"When we withdrew, my liege, we left it here," Warwick replied.

"Prince Hal has taken it away from here," Henry IV said. "Go, and seek him out. Is he so hasty to be King that he thinks that my sleep is my death? Find him, my Lord of Warwick; rebuke him and bring him here."

Warwick left to carry out his errand.

King Henry IV said, "This act of his joins forces with my disease, and it helps to end my life. See, sons, what things you are! How quickly nature falls into revolt when gold becomes her goal! A son ceases to love his father when the son begins to love gold. For this the foolish over-careful fathers have broken their sleep with thoughts, their brains with care, and their bones with industry. For this they have engrossed and piled up the rusty, tarnished, and morally corrupt heaps of strangely acquired gold. For this they have been thoughtful to instruct their sons in the arts and in martial exercises. When, like the bee, culling from every flower the virtuous sweets, our thighs packed with wax, our mouths filled with honey, we bring it to the hive, and, like the bees, we fathers are murdered for our pains. The gold and treasures that the father has gathered yield a bitter taste to him as he lies dying."

Warwick entered the room.

Henry IV asked him, "Now, where is he who will not wait even until his friend sickness has killed me?"

"My lord, I found Prince Hal in the next room," Warwick said, "washing with kindly tears his gentle cheeks, with such a demeanor steeped in great and deep sorrow that a tyrant, who never drank anything but blood, would, by beholding him, have washed his knife with gentle tears. Prince Hal is coming here."

"But why did he take away the crown?" Henry IV asked.

Carrying the crown, Prince Hal entered the room.

King Henry IV said, "Look, here he comes. Come here to me, Harry."

He said to the others in the room, "Depart from this chamber; leave us here alone."

They left the room.

"I never thought to hear you speak again," Prince Hal said.

"Your wish was father, Harry, to that thought." Henry IV said. "I stay too long by you; I weary you. You think that I live too long. Do you so hunger for my empty throne that you need to give yourself my honors before your hour is ripe and you lawfully inherit them? Foolish youth! You seek the greatness that will overwhelm you. Wait only a little while. My cloud of dignity is held from falling with so weak a wind that it will quickly drop: My day is dim. My Earthly greatness is as insubstantial as a cloud and will quickly dissipate, just as my breath is shallow and will soon stop. You have stolen that — my crown — which after some few hours would be yours without offence; and at my death you have sealed up my expectation and confirmed what I expected. Your life has shown that you do not love me, and your action just now will have me die entirely sure that you do not love me.

"You are hiding a thousand daggers in your thoughts, which you have sharpened on your stony heart, to stab at half an hour of my life. What! Can you not wait for half an hour and allow me to die of natural causes? Then leave and dig my grave yourself and order the merry bells to ring to your ears that you are crowned, not that I am dead. Let all the tears that should bedew my hearse be drops of balm — consecrated oil that will anoint you when you are crowned King — to sanctify your head. Only mix me with forgotten dust — give to the worms my body that gave you life.

"Pluck down my officers, and break my decrees. For now a time has come to mock at law and order. Harry the Fifth is crowned. Up with you, vanity! Down with everything good, royal state! All you wise counselors, go away! And to the English court assemble now, from every region, apes of idleness and fools with every kind of vice! Now, neighboring countries, purge yourself of your scum. Do you have a ruffian who swears, drinks to excess, dances wildly, revels throughout the night, robs, murders, and commits the oldest sins in the newest kind of ways? Be happy because that ruffian will trouble you no more; England shall double gild his treble guilt, and England shall give him office, honor, and might because the fifth Harry plucks from curbed license the muzzle of restraint, and the wild dog shall sink his teeth in every innocent, getting a taste of what shall be its prey.

"Oh, my poor Kingdom, sick with civil blows! Throughout my reign, my careful rule could not stop your riots. I tried my best to keep my Kingdom peaceful. What will my Kingdom do when riot is your caregiver? What will my Kingdom do when your King, who is supposed to be your caregiver, is himself a rioter? Oh, you will be a wilderness again; you will be peopled with wolves, your old inhabitants!"

"Oh, pardon me, my liege!" Prince Hal said. "Only my tears, the moist impediments that stopped my speech, kept me from stopping this heartfelt and deep rebuke before you with grief had spoken and I had heard the course of it so far."

Prince Hal placed the crown on a pillow by his father, knelt, and said, "There is your crown; and may He who wears the crown immortally — God — long guard it as your crown, not mine.

"If I value the crown as anything more than as your honor and as your renown, let me no more from this kneeling position rise. My most inward true and duteous spirit teaches me to kneel and bow to you.

"May God be my witness that when I here came in and found no sign that your majesty was breathing, cold struck my heart! If I am lying, let me in my present wildness die and never live to show the incredulous world the noble change that I have planned!

"Coming to look at you, and then thinking that you were dead, I was almost dead myself, my liege, to think that you were dead. I spoke to this crown as if it were sentient, and I thus upbraided it: 'The worry that you cause has fed upon the body of my father; therefore, you — the best of gold — are actually the worst of gold. Other gold, less fine in carat, is more precious. Potions containing gold are good medicine. But you, gold most fine, most honored, and most renowned, have eaten the King who wears you.' Thus, my most royal liege, accusing it, I put it on my head, to combat and fight with it, as with an enemy who had in front of me murdered my father — this is the battle faced by a true inheritor.

"But if wearing the crown did infect my blood with joy, or swell my thoughts to pride; if any rebel or vain spirit of mine did in the least welcome the crown's power, then let God forever keep it from my head and make me as the poorest vassal is who with awe and terror kneels to it!"

"My son, God put it in your mind to take it from here," King Henry IV said, "so that you could win the more your father's love by pleading so wisely in excuse of your taking the crown!

"Come here, Harry, and sit by my bed, and hear, I think, the very last advice that I shall ever breathe."

Prince Hal arose from his kneeling position and sat by his father.

Henry IV said, "God knows, my son, by what by-paths and indirect crooked ways I met and achieved this crown, and I myself know well how troublesome it has sat upon my head. To you it shall descend with better quiet, better reputation, and better right to its possession because all the stain of the achievement of the crown goes with me into the earth. It seemed in me only as an honor snatched with boisterous and violent hands, and many living people kept reminding me that they had assisted me as I won the crown. These people eventually quarreled with me and rebelled and caused bloodshed, wounding the peace. You can see that I have with peril put down all these bold dangers and rebellions. All my reign has been like a play that is only about disagreements and rebellion and battles.

"Now my death changes the mood of people's minds. I acquired the crown through deposing King Richard II, but you, Harry, will inherit the crown. That is how the people think that a crown ought to be acquired.

"However, although your claim to the crown is better than was my claim and has a firmer foundation, your claim is still not firm enough, since griefs are green and raw — the rebellion has only recently been put down. All my 'friends,' whom you must make your friends, have only recently had their stings and teeth taken out. By these friends' pernicious actions, I was first advanced to the crown. I was afraid that these friends' power could take the crown away from me. To prevent them from doing that, I cut them off and stopped their rebellion; and I had intended to lead many soldiers to the Holy Land in a crusade, lest their inactivity might make them look too closely at how I achieved the crown.

"Therefore, my Harry, make sure to keep giddy minds busy with foreign wars so that this warfare will wear away the memory of the former days. You do not want people to remember the deposition of King Richard II.

"I want to say more, but my lungs are so wasted that I do not have the strength to speak. How I came by the crown, may God forgive me, and may God grant that the crown will live with you in true peace!"

Prince Hal replied, "My gracious liege, you won the crown, wore it, kept it, and gave it to me; therefore, clear and plain and rightful must my possession be. I will rightfully maintain my possession of the crown with more than common care and pains against all the world."

Prince John of Lancaster entered the room.

Henry IV said, "Look, here comes my son Prince John of Lancaster."

"Health, peace, and happiness to my royal father!" Prince John of Lancaster said.

"You bring me happiness and peace, son John," Henry IV said. "But health, unfortunately, with youthful wings has flown away from this bare withered trunk. Now that I have seen you, my worldly business has come to an end."

He then asked, "Where is my Lord of Warwick?"

Prince Hal called, "My Lord of Warwick!"

Warwick and others entered the room.

"Does the room where I fainted have a particular name?" Henry IV asked Warwick.

"It is named Jerusalem, my noble lord."

"Praise be to God!" Henry IV said. "There my life must end. It was prophesied to me many years ago that I should die nowhere but in Jerusalem, which vainly I supposed to be the Holy Land. Carry me to that chamber. There I'll lie; in that Jerusalem shall Harry die."

# CHAPTER 5

## — 5.1 —

Falstaff was visiting Justice Shallow in his house in Gloucestershire. With them were Falstaff's page and Bardolph.

Justice Shallow said to Falstaff, "I swear by cock and pie, sir, you shall not go away from here tonight. I want you to be my guest tonight."

He called for a servant to come to him: "Davy!"

"You must excuse me, Master Robert Shallow," Falstaff replied.

Justice Shallow would not take no for an answer: "I will not excuse you; you shall not be excused; excuses shall not be admitted; there is no excuse that shall serve to excuse you; you shall not be excused."

He moved to the door and shouted, "Davy!"

Davy entered the room and said, "Here I am, sir."

"Davy, Davy, Davy, Davy, let me see, Davy; let me see, Davy; let me see," Justice Shallow said. "Tell William the cook to come here. Sir John, you shall not be excused."

Davy wanted Justice Shallow to make some business decisions. He showed him some papers and said, "Those legal writs cannot be served. Also, sir, shall we sow the headland with wheat?"

The headland is the strip of land where the plow turns. It cannot be sown until the rest of the field is sown.

"Sow it with red wheat," Justice Shallow replied.

Red wheat is a variety of wheat that is sown later than other varieties of wheat.

Justice Shallow said, "About William the cook: Are there any young pigeons that can be cooked?"

"Yes, sir," Davy replied. "Here is the blacksmith's bill for shoeing horses and for the plow blades."

"Add the figures, double-check them, and pay the bill," Justice Shallow said.

He added, "Sir John, you shall not be excused."

Davy said, "Now, sir, a new chain for the bucket is needed. Also, sir, do you mean to dock William's wages for the wine he lost the other day at Hinckley Fair?"

"Yes, dock his wages," Justice Shallow said. "Davy, tell William to cook some pigeons, a couple of short-legged hens because hens with short legs have more meat, a joint of mutton, and some pretty little tiny delicacies."

"Will the man of war — the Captain — stay all night, sir?"

Davy was referring to Falstaff. A man of war is a large ship, and Falstaff is a large man.

"Yes, Davy," Justice Shallow said. "I will treat him well: A friend in the court is better than a penny in the purse."

He whispered, "Treat his men well, Davy; they are arrant good-for-nothings, and will backbite."

"They will backbite no worse than they are backbitten, sir," Davy whispered back, "because they have marvelously foul linen and lice bite their backs."

"Well jested, Davy," Justice Shallow said. "Now go about your business, Davy."

"Please, sir," Davy said, "show favor to William Visor of Woncot in his lawsuit against Clement Perkes of the hill."

"There are many complaints, Davy, against that William Visor," Justice Shallow said. "That Visor is an arrant good-for-nothing — this I know."

"I grant your worship that he is a good-for-nothing, sir," Davy said, "but yet, God forbid, sir, that a good-for-nothing should not have some strings pulled at his friend's request. An honest man, sir, is able to speak for himself when a good-for-nothing is not. I have served your worship truly, sir, this eight years; and if I cannot once or twice in a quarter support a good-for-nothing against an honest man, I have only a very little credit with your worship. The good-for-nothing is my honest friend, sir; therefore, I beg your worship, show him some favor."

"I tell you that he shall suffer no wrong," Justice Shallow replied. "Go about your business, Davy."

Davy departed to do his duties.

"Where are you, Sir John?" Justice Shallow asked, looking around. Seeing Falstaff, he moved toward him and said to him, "Come, come, come, off with your boots."

He added, "Give me your hand, Master Bardolph."

He shook hands with Bardolph, who said, "I am glad to see your worship."

"I thank you with all my heart, kind Master Bardolph," Justice Shallow said. Then he said to the page, who was only a boy, "Welcome, my tall fellow."

He added, "Come, Sir John."

"I'll follow you, good Master Robert Shallow," Falstaff said.

He added, "Bardolph, look after our horses."

Bardolph and the page left to look after the horses, leaving Falstaff alone.

Falstaff said to himself, "If I were sawed into lengths, I would make four dozen bearded hermits' walking staffs — Justice Shallow is exactly the size of one such walking staff. It is a wonderful thing to see the close correspondence of his men's spirits and his. By observing him, his servants learn how to act like foolish justices. By talking to his servants, he learns to act like a justice-like servant. Their spirits are so alike because of their close partnership that they act like so many wild geese that fly together in close formation. If I needed a favor from Master Shallow, I would court his servants by pretending to be friends with their master. If I needed a favor from his servants, I would curry favor with Master Shallow by flattering him by saying that no man could better command his servants.

"It is certain that either wise bearing or ignorant carriage is caught, as men take diseases, one from another. If you wish to be wise, seek the company of the wise. If you wish to be foolish, seek the company of the foolish. Men need to take heed of their company. As a man is, so is his company. I will get so much comedic material from observing this Shallow that I will keep Prince Harry continually laughing for the length of time that it takes six fashions to go out of fashion. That length of time is one year, which is the length of four terms held at the Inns of Court, or of two legal actions, and Prince Hal shall laugh without intermissions.

"A lie told with a slight oath that it is true and a jest told with a straight face will do much to cause laughter in a young fellow who has never had a backache! Prince Hal will laugh until his face wrinkles like a wet cloak that was carelessly rolled up into a ball and allowed to dry!"

Justice Shallow called, "Sir John!"

"I am coming, Master Shallow," Falstaff called back. "I am coming, Master Shallow."

Warwick and the Lord Chief Justice talked together in the palace at Westminster. The Lord Chief Justice expected trouble after the death of King Henry IV. Prince Hal would become King Henry V, and Prince Hal and the Lord Chief Justice had earlier had a serious disagreement. Prince Hal had wanted one of his lowlife friends to escape being punished for a crime, the Lord Chief Justice had refused to be less than just, Prince Hal had struck the Lord Chief Justice, and the Lord Chief Justice had ordered Prince Hal to be put in prison.

"How are you now, Lord Chief Justice?" Warwick asked. "Where are you going?"

"How is the King?" the Lord Chief Justice asked.

"Exceedingly well; his cares are now all ended."

"He is not dead, I hope."

"He has walked the way of nature, and in our human world he lives no more," Warwick said. "Now he lives in another world."

"I wish that his majesty had called me to go with him," the Lord Chief Justice said. "The service that I truly and faithfully did for him during his life has left me open to many injuries."

"Indeed I think that the young King — Henry V — does not like you."

"I know that he does not, and I am preparing myself to meet the condition and temper of the times, which cannot look more hideously upon me than I have imagined."

Three of the Kings' sons — Prince John of Lancaster, Prince Thomas of Clarence, and Prince Humphrey of Gloucester — entered the room. So did Westmoreland and some others.

"Here come the grieving sons of dead Harry," Warwick said. "I wish that the living Harry — the new Henry V — had the character of the worst of these three gentlemen! How many nobles then should hold their places of respect instead of bowing down to people of vile character, the way that a honest ship is forced to lower its sails to pirates."

"I am afraid that law and order will be overturned in our country!" the Lord Chief Justice said.

Prince John of Lancaster said, "Good morning, cousin Warwick, good morning."

Prince Thomas of Clarence and Prince Humphrey of Gloucester said, "Good morning, cousin."

Prince John of Lancaster said, "We meet like men who have forgotten how to speak."

"We remember how to speak," Warwick said, "but the topic of our conversation is much too sad and serious to allow for much talking."

"Well, may peace be with him who has made us mourn," Prince John of Lancaster said.

"May peace be with us, lest we mourn more than we do now!" the Lord Chief Justice said.

"My good Lord Chief Justice," Prince Humphrey of Gloucester said, "you have lost a friend indeed, and I dare to swear that you are not borrowing that face that shows sorrow. I am sure that you feel real sorrow for my father's death."

"Though no man knows what will happen to him as a result of having a new King," Prince John of Lancaster said, "you have the most reason to expect to be badly treated. I am sorry about that; I wish that it were otherwise."

"Well, you must now speak only good things about Sir John Falstaff," Prince Thomas of Clarence said. "I know that this goes entirely against your character. You know Sir John's many and great faults."

"Sweet Princes, what I did, I honorably did," the Lord Chief Justice said. "I was led by the impartial conduct of my soul. I will never beg for a ragged pardon that I know will not be granted to me. If the truth and my upright innocence fail me, I will go to the King my master who is dead, and tell him who has sent me after him."

"Here comes the Prince," Warwick said.

Prince Hal, who was very soon to be crowned King Henry V, entered the room with some of his attendants.

The Lord Chief Justice said, "Good morning, and may God save your majesty!"

Prince Hal, who knew that people were concerned about his future rule because he had been so wild as a young man, said, "This new and gorgeous garment, majesty, sits not so easily on me as you must think. Brothers, you mix your sadness about my father's death with some fear about my future rule. This is the English, not the Turkish court; an Amurath is not succeeding another Amurath. Instead, a Harry is succeeding another Harry."

Prince Hal was referring to cruel Turkish rulers. In 1574, when Murad III, aka Amurath, succeeded his father as Emperor of the Turks, he had all of his brothers killed so that they could not challenge him for the throne. In 1596, Mehmet III, who succeeded Murad III, did the same to his brothers for the same reason.

Prince Hal said to the men, who were wearing black in mourning, "Yet be sad, good brothers, because, truly, it very well becomes you. Sorrow appears so royally in you that I will in deadly earnest put the fashion on and wear sorrow in my heart. Therefore, be sad and mourn, but be aware, good brothers, that the reason for your — and my — sadness and grief is one that is a joint burden laid upon us all. Do not be sad and grieve because I will be King. By Heaven, I assure you that I'll be your father and your brother, too. Let me bear your love, and I will also bear your cares. Yet weep because Harry is dead; and so will I. But another Harry — me — lives, and he shall convert those tears into hours of happiness. Each tear you shed now shall result in an hour of happiness later."

"We hope for no less from your majesty," the three Princes said.

"You all are looking strangely at me," Prince Hal said.

He then said to the Lord Chief Justice, "You are looking at me most strangely of all. You are, I think, convinced that I do not like you."

"I am convinced that if I am judged rightly," the Lord Chief Justice said, "your majesty has no just cause to hate me."

"No!" Prince Hal said. "How might a Prince of my great hopes of ascending the throne forget the great indignities that you laid upon me? What! You berated, rebuked, and roughly sent to prison the immediate heir of the King of England! Is this easy to forget? May this be washed in Lethe, the river of forgetfulness in the afterlife, and forgotten? Do you expect me to wash myself in Lethe and forget that you ever did these things to me?"

"When I did those things," the Lord Chief Justice said, "I used the authority given to me by your father. I was the representative of the King. The image of his power lay then in me, and I had his authority to administer his law. While I was busy working for the commonwealth, your highness was pleased to forget my position, and the majesty and power of law and justice — the image of the King whom I represented. You struck me on my head — my very seat of judgment. Therefore, you were an offender to your father — by offending me, his representative, you offended your father. Therefore, I boldly used my authority and my power to commit you to prison.

"If you regard my deed as ill, then I hope that you, who will now wear the crown, will be happy to have a son who will regard your decrees as worthless, who will pluck down justice from your bench that should inspire awe, who will trip the course of law and blunt the sword that guards the peace and safety of your person. Nay, more, I hope that you, who will now wear the crown, will be happy to have a son who will spurn your most royal image and mock your workings in a second body. I hope that you, who will now wear the crown, will be happy to have a son who mocks you and mocks your representative, both of whom are responsible for bringing justice to your Kingdom.

"Pretend that you are now the father and imagine that you have a son. Hear your own son greatly profane your dignity. See your most important laws greatly slighted. Behold yourself being so disdained by a son. And then imagine me taking your part and using the power that you have invested in me to quietly silence and correct your son. Carefully think about this, and then pronounce a sentence against me. And, in your position as King, tell me what I have done that misbecame my place, my person, or my liege's sovereignty. Tell me, in your position as King, what I have done wrong."

"You are right, Lord Chief Justice," Prince Hal said, "and you weigh this matter well. You have carefully thought about what is right for you to do. Therefore, continue to bear the balance and the sword of justice. And I wish that your honors may increase, until you live to see a son of mine offend you and then obey you, as I did. I want you to treat my son as you treated me. If you do that, I shall live to speak my father's words: 'Happy am I, who have a man so bold, who dares give justice to my own son; and I am not less happy in having a son who would deliver up his greatness into the hands of justice.' My father wanted a son who would obey the laws despite his being King. You sent me to prison. Because you did what was right and just, I commit into your hand the sword — unstained by any perversion of justice — that you have been bearing. I do this with this proviso: that you continue to act with the same bold, just, and impartial spirit that you have used to give the younger, wilder me the justice I deserved. Here is my hand."

They shook hands.

Prince Hal continued, "You shall be like a father to my youth. My voice shall say the words that you whisper in my ear, and I will stoop and make myself humble and act in accordance with your well-practiced wise directions."

He then said to his brothers, "And, all you Princes, believe me, please. My father has gone wildly and excitedly into his grave, because in his tomb lie my violent and wild desires. My ignoble desires have been buried with my father's body. But my father's serious spirit lives on in me. I will use that serious spirit to mock the expectation of the world, to frustrate prophecies, and to raze out rotten opinion, which has judged me according to the wildness I showed in my youth. Everyone expects me to be a wild and bad King who does not respect justice, but I will show the world that those people are wrong. The tide of blood in me has proudly flowed in vanity until now. Now it turns and ebbs back to the sea, where it shall mingle with the mighty ocean and flow henceforth in formal majesty.

"Now we will call our high court of Parliament, and we will choose such limbs of noble counsel, that the great body of our state — England — will rank among the best-governed nations. I want England to be prepared for war, or peace, or both at once; I want them to be things acquainted and familiar to us so that we will know how to deal well with them. In my government, you, Lord Chief Justice, will have a foremost hand.

"Once our coronation has been done, we will summon, as I previously mentioned, all the members of our Parliament, and, if God endorses my good intentions, no Prince nor peer shall have just cause to say, 'May God shorten Harry's happy life by even one day!'"

In Justice Shallow's orchard in Gloucestershire were Falstaff, Justice Shallow, Justice Silence, Davy, Bardolph, and the page. They had eaten the evening meal, and now Justice Shallow wanted his guests to talk together and eat snacks in his orchard.

Justice Shallow said to Falstaff, "No, you must and shall see my orchard, where, in an arbor, we will eat a last year's pippin of my own grafting, with a dish of delicacies made with caraway seeds, and so forth."

Last year's pippins were apples that were eaten after they had been stored for a year.

He added, "Come, cousin Silence, and after we eat and drink, we will go to bed and sleep."

"By God," Falstaff said, "you have here a good and rich dwelling."

"It is poor, poor, poor," Justice Shallow replied. "We are beggars all, beggars all, Sir John. But at least we have good air. Spread the tablecloth, Davy; spread it out."

Davy put the tablecloth on the table and started setting out utensils and glasses and dishes of food.

"Well done, Davy," Justice Shallow said.

"This Davy serves you well," Falstaff said. "He is your serving-man and your steward."

"He is a good servant, a good servant, a very good servant, Sir John," Justice Shallow said. "By the Mass, I have drunk too much wine at supper. Davy is a good servant. Now sit down; now sit down. Come, Justice Silence."

Justice Silence sang, "Do nothing but eat and enjoy ourselves.

"And praise God for the merry year;

"When flesh is cheap and females dear,

"And lusty lads roam here and there

"So merrily,

"And all the while so merrily."

"There's a merry heart!" Falstaff said. "Good Master Silence, I'll drink to you and wish you health soon."

"Give Master Bardolph some wine, Davy," Justice Shallow said.

"Sweet sir, sit," Davy said. "I'll be with you soon. Most sweet sir, sit."

Davy said to Falstaff's page, who was with Bardolph, "Master page, good master page, sit. *Proface*! What you want in meat, we'll have in drink. What you lack in food, we will make up in drink. You must endure it; what is in the heart is everything. Good wishes count for much."

Davy exited to get more refreshments.

*Proface* comes from the Italian *Buon pro vi faccia*, which means, "May it do you good."

"Be merry, Master Bardolph; and, my little soldier page there, be merry," Justice Shallow said.

Justice Silence sang, "Be merry, be merry, my wife has everything.

"For women are shrews, both short and tall.

"It is merry in hall when beards wag all,

"And welcome merry Shrove-tide.

"Be merry, be merry."

Shrove-tide is a time of merry-making before the beginning of Lent, during which many Christians practice self-denial.

Falstaff said to Justice Shallow, "I did not think Master Silence had been a man of this mettle. I did not think that he was a merry-maker."

Justice Silence heard him and said, "Who, I? I have been merry twice and once before now. This is the fourth time in my life that I have made merry."

Davy put some apples on the table and said to Bardolph, "There's a dish of leather-coats for you."

The apples were russet apples, whose rough skins resembled leather.

Davy was treating Bardolph well — very well.

"Davy!" Justice Shallow said.

"Your worship!" Davy replied. "I'll be with you right away."

He asked Bardolph, "A cup of wine, sir?"

Justice Silence sang, "A cup of wine that's brisk and fine.

"And drink unto thee, leman mine;

"And a merry heart lives long-a."

A leman is a sweetheart.

"Well done, Master Silence," Falstaff said.

Justice Silence sang, "And we shall be merry,

"Now comes in the sweetest part of the night."

"Health and long life to you, Master Silence," Falstaff said in a toast.

Justice Silence sang, "Fill the cup, and let it come;

"I'll pledge you a mile to the bottom."

In the song, Judge Silence pledged to drink a toast in its entirety even if the cup of wine was so deep that it was a mile to its bottom.

"Honest Bardolph, you are welcome," Justice Shallow said. "If you want anything, and you will not call for it, then do without because all you have to do is ask for it."

He added, "Welcome, page, my little tiny thief — and welcome indeed, too. I'll drink to Master Bardolph, and to all the gallants — the Spanish *caballeros* — about London."

"I hope to see London once before I die," Davy said.

"If I might see you there, Davy —" Bardolph began.

Justice Shallow interrupted, "By the Mass, you'll empty a goblet containing a quart of wine together, won't you! Won't you, Master Bardolph?"

"Yes, sir, we will share a pottle-pot," Bardolph said.

Bardolph had doubled the quantity that he and Davy would drink. A pottle-pot held two quarts of wine.

"By God's eyelids, I thank you," Justice Shallow said. "The rascal Davy will stick by you, I can assure you that. He will not drop out when you drink; he is true bred and true blue."

"And I'll stick by him, sir," Bardolph replied.

"Why, spoken like a King," Justice Shallow said. "Lack for nothing; be merry."

They heard knocking.

"See who is at the door!" Justice Shallow said. "Who is knocking?"

Davy exited.

Seeing Justice Silence drinking, Falstaff said to him, "Why, now you have done me right."

Justice Silence sang, "Do me right,

"And dub me knight: Samingo."

Samingo was Monsieur Mingo, a character in a French drinking song. *Mingo* is Latin for "I urinate."

Justice Silence asked, "Isn't that right?"

Falstaff replied, "That's right."

"Is that so?" Justice Silence said. "Well, then, say an old man can do something."

Davy returned and said to Justice Shallow, "If it please your worship, a man named Pistol has come from the court with news."

"From the court!" Falstaff said. "Let him come in."

Pistol walked into the orchard.

"How are you, Pistol?" Falstaff said.

"Sir John, may God save you!" Pistol replied.

"What wind blew you here, Pistol?" Falstaff said.

"Not the ill wind that blows no man to good," Pistol said. "Sweet knight, you are now one of the greatest men in this realm."

Justice Silence, who understood "greatest" to mean "fattest," said, "By Mother Mary, I think he is, except for the good Puff of Barson."

"Puff!" Pistol shouted, "Puff in your teeth, you most forsworn and base coward!"

He added, "Sir John, I am your Pistol and your friend, and helter-skelter have I rode to you, and tidings do I bring and lucky joys and golden times and happy news of value."

"Please, tell me your news as if you were an ordinary man of this world and not a hero in a play," Falstaff said.

Pistol continued to use extravagant language: "A *foutre* for the world and worldlings base! I speak of Africa and golden joys."

"*Foutre*" was French for "f**k."

Imitating Pistol's extravagant language, Falstaff said, "Oh, base Ass-syrian knight, what is your news? Let King Cophetua know the truth thereof."

Cophetua was a King who married a beggar; a popular song told this tale.

Justice Silence sang, "And let Robin Hood, Will Scarlet, and Friar John know the truth."

Pistol shouted, "Shall dunghill curs confront the Helicons? And shall good news be baffled? Then, Pistol, lay your head in Furies' lap."

As usual, Pistol's knowledge of mythology was somewhat muddled.

The Muses resided on Mount Helicon; Pistol thought that "Helicons" was an alternate name for the Muses. Most people would not think of laying their head on the lap of the Furies, who were terrifying goddesses of vengeance.

"Honest gentleman, I do not know your social status," Justice Shallow said.

"Why then, lament therefore," Pistol said.

"Pardon me, sir," Justice Shallow said. "If, sir, you come with news from the court, I take it that there are only two things you can do. You can either tell your news, or you can not tell your news. I have, sir, under the King, a position of some authority."

"Under which King, Besonian?" Pistol shouted. "Speak, or die."

By "Besonian," Pistol meant the Italian *bisogno* or *bisognoso*, a beggar with no redeeming features, either physical or mental.

"Under King Harry," Justice Shallow replied.

"Harry the Fourth? Or the Fifth?"

"Harry the Fourth."

"A *foutre* for your office!" Pistol shouted at Justice Shallow.

Now that King Henry IV was dead, Justice Shallow might lose his position of Justice of the Peace.

Pistol said, "Sir John, your tender lambkin — Prince Hal — now is King! Harry the Fifth's the man! I speak the truth: When Pistol lies, do this" — he made an obscene gesture — "and fig me, like the bragging Spaniard."

The fig of Spain was an obscene gesture in which the thumb was thrust between the index and the middle finger.

"What! Is the old King dead?" Falstaff asked.

"He is as dead as a nail in a door," Pistol replied. "The things I speak are true."

Falstaff's dream had come true. King Henry IV was dead. His mind flooded with thoughts about what was to follow that death. His companion, Prince Hal, would become King Henry V. With such a powerful friend, Falstaff could run wild, breaking every law and looting the royal treasury.

He shouted, "Let's go, Bardolph! Saddle my horse!"

He added, "Master Robert Shallow, choose whatever office you want in England — it will be yours. Pistol, I will double-charge you with dignities. I intend to reward all my friends by giving them power and prestige."

"Oh, joyful day!" Bardolph said. "I would not take a knighthood for my future fortune!"

"See! I do bring good news!" Pistol said.

Meanwhile in London, Prince Hal was mourning the death of his father.

Having drunk too much wine, Justice Silence had fallen asleep.

"Carry Master Silence to bed," Falstaff ordered. "Master Shallow, my Lord Shallow — be whatever you want to be; take whatever title you want; I am Fortune's steward and will provide — put on your boots! We'll ride all night! Oh, sweet Pistol! Saddle the horses, Bardolph!"

Bardolph left to get everything ready for them to ride all night back to London.

Falstaff said, "Come, Pistol, tell me more, and think about what you want me to give to you. Put on your boots, Master Shallow. I know that the young King wants to see me. Let us take any man's horses; the laws of England are at my commandment."

Falstaff wanted to take any man's horses. He meant that he wanted to press them in the King's service and avoid paying money for them. His belief that "the laws of England are at my commandment" was shocking because no one, not even the Prince of Wales or the King, ought to be above the law.

Falstaff shouted, "Blessed are they who have been my friends, and woe to the Lord Chief Justice!"

Pistol shouted, "Let vile vultures seize on his lungs also!"

Pistol was willing for the Lord Chief Justice to suffer torments such as Prometheus of antiquity had suffered. Prometheus had given human beings fire and the knowledge to control it. As punishment for Prometheus' good deed to Humankind, Zeus, the Greek King of the gods, chained him and sent two vultures each day to eat his liver.

Pistol said, "'Where is the life that late I led?' say they. Why, here it is; welcome these pleasant days!"

On a street in London, some Beadles — officers of the law who handled and punished petty offences — had arrested Mistress Quickly and Doll Tearsheet, who were not happy about being arrested.

"No, you arrant good-for-nothing," Mistress Quickly shouted at a Beadle. "I wish to God that I would die, so that I might have you hanged for causing my death. You have dislocated my shoulder!"

The first Beadle said, "The Constables have delivered her — Doll Tearsheet — over to me; and she shall be whipped soon enough, I promise her. She will get a bellyful of whipping. There has been a man or two lately killed about her."

Apparently, he meant that two men had been fighting over Doll Tearsheet, and one man had killed the other. Also apparently, the murder had taken place in Mistress Quickly's tavern. Whipping was a common punishment for prostitutes.

"Nut-hook, nut-hook, you lie!" Doll Tearsheet said.

A nut-hook was a slang term for a Beadle. Nut-hooks were used to hook the branches of a nut tree and pull them down so that the nuts could be harvested. Nut-hooks caught the branches, and Beadles caught petty criminals.

Doll Tearsheet continued to shout: "Come on! I will tell you what, you damned sallow-faced rascal, if the child I am pregnant with miscarries, you will wish that you had hit your own mother instead of harassing me, you paper-faced villain!"

"Oh, Lord," Mistress Quickly said, "I wish that Sir John were here! He would make this a bloody day for somebody."

Mistress Quickly thought that Falstaff would be a powerful man in England now Prince Hal was King. So did Falstaff.

Mistress Quickly added, "But I pray to God that the fruit of her womb does miscarry!"

The first Beadle replied, "If it does miscarry, you shall have a dozen cushions again; you have only eleven now."

The Beadles — and Mistress Quickly — knew that Doll Tearsheet was not pregnant. She had stuffed a cushion under her dress in order to appear pregnant. She was hoping for better treatment and a lesser punishment from the Beadles.

The first Beadle added, "Come, I order you both to go with me; for the man is dead whom you and Pistol beat in your midst."

"I'll tell you what, you thin man in a censer," Doll Tearsheet shouted, "I will have you soundly beaten for this — you blue-bottle rogue, you filthy famished correctioner. If you are not beaten, I'll forswear skirts."

The first Beadle was a very thin man. By "thin man in a censer," Doll Tearsheet was referring to a figure engraved on a perfuming pan. By "blue-bottle rogue," she meant that the first Beadle was a rogue wearing a blue coat — police officers wore blue. A "correctioner" was an officer in charge of whipping prostitutes.

"Come, come, you she-knight-errant, come," the Beadle ordered.

Doll Tearsheet was a female night-errant. She committed sins at night.

"Oh, God, that right should thus overcome might!" Mistress Quickly mourned.

She frequently erred in her speech; she meant to bewail might overcoming right. However, her statement really did have some degree of accuracy — right was winning.

Mistress Quickly added, "Well, of sufferance comes ease. Suffering builds character."

"Come, you rogue, come," Doll Tearsheet said to the first Beadle. "Take me to a justice."

"Yes, come, you starved bloodhound," Mistress Quickly added.

"You are death! You are bones!" Doll Tearsheet said to the first Beadle.

Mistress Quickly added, "You are a skeleton!"

"Come, you thin thing," Doll Tearsheet said. "Come, you rascal."

"Very well," the first Beadle said, and he led them to a Justice of the Peace.

In a public street near Westminster Abbey, two men were strewing rushes, plants that were usually used as floor coverings, on the street. King Henry V was being crowned, and he would be traveling on this street soon.

The first man said, "More rushes, more rushes."

The second man said, "The trumpets have sounded twice."

The first man said, "It will be two o'clock before they come from the coronation. Hurry! Hurry!"

They left, and Falstaff, Justice Shallow, Pistol, Bardolph, and the page arrived.

Falstaff said, "Stand here by me, Master Robert Shallow; I will make the King show favor to you. I will look him directly in the face as he goes by. Watch the facial expression he will give to me."

Falstaff expected a good reception from the King; however, he did not plan to show the King the respect that was due to the King. Citizens on the street were expected to bow their heads respectfully as the King went by. Falstaff believed that he need not do that. He expected the new King — the former Prince Hal — to allow him to do whatever he wanted to do. Falstaff wanted wealth and honor for himself and his friends, and he wanted to punish the Lord Chief Justice.

"God bless your lungs, good knight," Pistol said. He expected Falstaff to shout to the King so that the King would see him.

"Come here, Pistol," Falstaff said. "Stand behind me."

He then said to Justice Shallow, "Oh, if only I had had time to have ordered new clothing to be made for myself in honor of the King, I would have spent the thousand pounds I borrowed from you. But it does not matter; the travel-stained clothing I am wearing shows how eager I was to see the new King. It implies the zeal I had to see him."

"That is true," Justice Shallow said.

"It shows my earnestness of affection and how much I love him —" Falstaff said.

"That is true," Justice Shallow said.

"My devotion —" Falstaff said.

"That is true, true, true," Justice Shallow said.

"It shows that I rode day and night," Falstaff said, "and it shows that I did not think, remember, or have enough patience to pause and change into clean clothing —" Falstaff said.

"That is best, no doubt," Justice Shallow said.

"So here I stand stained with travel, and sweating with desire to see him," Falstaff said. "It shows that I am thinking of nothing else, I am putting all other affairs aside, as if there were nothing else to be done except to see him."

Pistol said, "It is *semper idem*, for *obsque hoc nihil est*; it is all in every part."

Pistol knew a little Latin. *Semper idem* means "always the same." By *obsque* Pistol meant *absque*; *absque hoc nihil est* means "apart from this, there is nothing."

"That is true, indeed," Justice Shallow said.

"My knight, I will inflame your noble liver and make you rage," Pistol said. "I will tell you something that will make you angry. Your Doll Tearsheet, who is the Helen of Troy of your noble thoughts, is suffering base imprisonment in a pestilential prison. She was haled thither by a most working-class and dirty hand. Rouse up revenge from ebon den — dark Hell — with fell and dangerous Alecto's snake, because your Doll Tearsheet is in jail. Pistol speaks nothing but the truth."

Alecto was one of the Furies, goddesses of vengeance. Her hair was snakes.

"I will deliver her," Falstaff said confidently. "I will make sure that she is set free."

Trumpets sounded; the new King — Henry V — was coming.

"There roared the sea, and trumpet-clangor sounds," Pistol said.

King Henry V and several other men, including the Chief Lord Justice, arrived.

Falstaff and Pistol did not behave the way that the King's loyal subjects ought to behave. They should have bowed their heads respectfully; instead, they looked at and shouted at the King as if they were in a bar carousing together.

"God save your grace, King Hal!" Falstaff shouted. "My royal Hal!"

"The Heavens guard and keep you, most royal imp of fame!" Pistol shouted.

"God save you, my sweet boy!" Falstaff said.

King Henry V knew that he had to reject Falstaff; otherwise, Falstaff would flout law and order and would rob the royal treasury. However, he was not looking forward to it and preferred to do it in private. He hoped that the Lord Chief Justice could take care of the situation for now.

King Henry V said, "My Lord Chief Justice, speak to that vain and foolish man and make him behave properly."

The Lord Chief Justice said to Falstaff, "Have you lost your wits? Don't you know to whom you are speaking?"

Falstaff shoved the Lord Chief Justice aside and shouted at Henry V, "My King! My Jove! I speak to you, my heart!"

This was the moment that King Henry V had to choose between the rule of law and the no rule of disorder. Who would be his chief counselor? Would it be the Lord Chief Justice, who would advise him well and obey the laws of England and do what was best for England? Or would it be Falstaff, who would advise him ill and disobey the laws of England and do what was best for Falstaff? Falstaff was forcing the King to make this decision on a public street with many witnesses.

King Henry V looked at Falstaff and said, "I know thee not, old man. Fall to your knees and pray. How ill white hairs become a fool and jester! I have long dreamed of such a kind of man as you — very swelled by eating to excess, very old, and very profane. But, now that I am awake, I despise my dream. Henceforward, make your body less in size, and work to strengthen your virtue. Stop gormandizing; know that the grave gapes for you three times wider than for other men."

Like Falstaff, King Henry V knew the Bible. When he said "I know thee not," he was referencing Matthew 25:1-13. These were words the Lord spoke to the foolish virgins.

Falstaff opened his mouth to speak, but Henry V cut him off: "Reply not to me with a fool-born jest. You were born a fool, and only fools can bear your jests. Presume not that I am the thing I was; for God knows, and soon the world will perceive, that I have turned away and rejected my former self. So will I turn away and reject those who kept me company.

"When you hear that I am as I was used to be, approach me, and you shall be what you used to be — the tutor and the feeder of my riotous behavior. Until then, I banish you, on pain of death, as I have done the rest of my misleaders.

Do not come as close to our royal person as ten miles — if you disobey this command, you will die.

"I will allow you to receive a pension so that you can pay for the necessities of life; that way, lack of means will not force you to do evil. And, when and if we hear that you have reformed yourselves, we will, according to your strengths and qualities, give you advancement."

King Henry V said to the Lord Chief Justice, "It is your task, my lord, to see that what I just said is carried out. Let's go."

King Henry V, the Lord Chief Justice, and the King's attendants exited.

Falstaff said, "Master Shallow, I owe you a thousand pounds."

"Yes, you do," Justice Shallow said, "and I beg you to let me have it so that I can take it home with me."

"That can hardly be, Master Shallow," said Falstaff, who had not yet spent the money. "Do not grieve at this; I shall be sent for in private to go to the King. Look, he must seem to reject me in public; he will treat me differently in private. Do not be afraid that I will not use my influence to get advancements for you; I will yet be the man who shall make you a great man."

Justice Shallow joked, "I cannot see how you can make me a great man, unless you should give me your jacket and stuff it with straw. I beg you, good Sir John, let me have five hundred of my thousand pounds."

Say what you will about Falstaff, he was not the kind of man to whom you ought to lend money — or allow to advise you how to run a country.

Ignoring the request, Falstaff said, "Sir, I will be as good as my word. This that you heard was only a color — a pretense."

Justice Shallow joked, "A color that I fear you will die in, Sir John. You will die with a hangman's collar — a noose — around your neck."

Justice Shallow had actually made a double pun. "Die" also meant "dye" — Falstaff would die in a hangman's collar while wearing a dyed color.

"Fear no colors," Falstaff punned back. "Colors" are the flags of the enemy, and so Falstaff was saying, "Fear no enemy."

He added, "Come with me and let us go to dinner. Come, Lieutenant Pistol; come, Bardolph. I shall be sent for soon, at night."

Falstaff had verbally given Ancient, aka Ensign, Pistol a promotion to Lieutenant; he was still hopeful of being a great man in England with the patronage of King Henry V.

Prince John of Lancaster, the Lord Chief Justice, and several officers of the law came over to Falstaff and the others. King Henry V was thinking ahead. He knew that Falstaff would still try to be his advisor, and he wanted to make it very clear to Falstaff that that was not going to happen. Or perhaps it was the Lord Chief Justice or Prince John of Lancaster who was thinking ahead.

The Lord Chief Justice ordered the law officers,

"Arrest and take Sir John Falstaff to the Fleet Prison and detain him there. Take all his company along with him."

"My lord, my lord —" Falstaff started to say.

The Lord Chief Justice cut him off: "I cannot speak to you now. I will hear your case soon."

He said to the law officers, "Take them away."

Pistol said one of his mottos: "*Si fortune me tormenta, spero contenta.* [If fortune torments me, hope comforts me.]"

The law officers took Falstaff and his companions to prison, leaving behind Prince John of Lancaster and the Lord Chief Justice.

Prince John of Lancaster said, "I like this fair proceeding of the King's. He intends that his former companions shall all be very well provided for, but he has banished all of them until their conversations appear more wise and modest to the world."

"They are definitely banished," the Lord Chief Justice said.

"The King has called his Parliament, my lord," Prince John of Lancaster said.

"Yes, he has."

"I will lay odds that, before the end of this year, we will bear our swords that have been used in civil wars and our native fire as far as France. I heard a bird so sing, whose music, I think, pleased the King.

"Come, shall we go?"

They went to the Parliament.

# EPILOGUE

Note: In the Epilogue, a person would appear after a play was over and speak to the audience, usually to ask for applause, but sometimes to convey information. This epilogue contains three paragraphs, but probably never would all three paragraphs be spoken together. A particular performance of *2 Henry IV* would have an epilogue of one or two of the paragraphs below, but probably never all three. Sometimes, a dance performance would follow the end of a play.

**Paragraph #1: Possibly Spoken by the Playwright:**

"First I will tell you what my fear is, then I will bow to you with courtesy, and last I will make my speech. My fear is your displeasure and your dislike of this play; my courtesy is my duty to you; and the purpose of my speech is to beg your pardons. If you look for a good speech now, you undo me because what I have to say is of my own making; and what indeed I should say will, I fear, prove my own marring. But to the purpose, and so to the venture. As you very well know, I was lately here on stage at the end of a play that displeased the audience, and I asked for your forgiveness for it and I promised you a better play. I meant indeed to repay you with this play, which, if it is like a business venture that goes badly, I will break my promise and go bankrupt, and you, my gentle creditors, will lose what I promised you. Here I promised you that I would be, and here I commit my body to your mercies. Forgive me some of my debt and I will pay you some of what I owe you and, as most debtors do, I will promise you infinitely and over and over to pay back the rest of what I owe you someday. I now kneel down before you to pray for the Queen."

**Paragraph #2: Spoken by a Dancer:**

"If my tongue cannot entreat you to acquit me, will you command me to use my legs? Yet that would be only a light payment, to lightly dance out of your debt. But a good conscience will make any possible satisfaction, and so would I. All the gentlewomen here have forgiven me. If the gentlemen will not forgive me, then the gentlemen do not agree with the gentlewomen, which has never been seen before in such an assembly."

**Paragraph #3: Spoken by a Dancer:**

"One word more, I beg you. If you are not too much cloyed with fat meat, our humble author will continue the story in another play, *Henry V*, with Sir

John Falstaff in it, and make you merry with fair Katharine of France. In France, for all I know, Falstaff shall die of a sweat, unless he is already killed with your hard opinions. Oldcastle died a martyr, and Falstaff is not Oldcastle. My tongue is weary; when my legs are weary, too, I will bid you good night."

# APPENDIX A: BRIEF HISTORICAL BACKGROUND

**KING EDWARD I: 1272-1307**

Edward Longshanks fought and defeated the Welsh chieftains, and he made his eldest son the Prince of Wales. He won victories against the Scots, and he brought the coronation stone from Scone to Westminster.

**KING EDWARD II: 1307-deposed 1327**

At the Battle of Bannockburn in 1314, the Scots defeated his army. His wife and her lover, Mortimer, deposed him. According to legend, he was murdered in Berkeley Castle by means of a red-hot poker thrust up his anus.

**KING EDWARD III: 1327-1377**

Son of King Edward II, he reigned for a long time — 50 years. Because he wanted to conquer Scotland and France, he started the Hundred Years War in 1338. King Edward III and his eldest son, Edward the Black Prince, won important victories against the French in the Battle of Crécy (1346) and the Battle of Poitiers (1356).

One of King Edward III's sons was John of Gaunt, first Duke of Lancaster.

Another of King Edward III's sons was Edmund of Langley, first Duke of York.

During his reign, the Black Death — the bubonic plague — struck in 1348-1350 and killed half of England's population.

**KING RICHARD II: 1377-deposed 1399**

King Richard II was the son of Edward the Black Prince. In 1381, Wat Tyler led the Peasants Revolt, which was suppressed. King Richard II sent Henry, Duke of Lancaster, into exile and seized Henry's estates, but in 1399 Henry, Duke of Lancaster, returned from exile and deposed King Richard II, thereby becoming King Henry IV. In 1400, King Richard II was murdered in Pontefract Castle, which is also known as Pomfret Castle.

# HOUSE OF LANCASTER

**KING HENRY IV: 1399-1413**

Henry, Duke of Lancaster, was the son of John of Gaunt, who was the third son of King Edward III. He was born at Bolingbroke Castle and so was also known as Henry of Bolingbroke. Returning from exile in France to reclaim his estates, he deposed King Richard II. He spent the 13 years of his reign putting down rebellions and defending himself against those who would assassinate or depose him. The Welshman Owen Glendower and the English Percy family were among those who fought against him. King Henry IV died at the age of 45.

**KING HENRY V: 1413-1422**

The son of King Henry IV, King Henry V renewed the war with France. He and his army defeated the French at the Battle of Agincourt (1415) despite being heavily outnumbered. He married Catherine of Valoise, the daughter of the French King, but he died before becoming King of France. He left behind a 10-month-old son, who became King Henry VI.

**KING HENRY VI: 1422-deposed 1461; briefly returned to the throne in 1470-1471**

The Hundred Years War ended in 1453; the English lost all land in France except for Calais, a port city. After King Henry VI suffered an attack of mental illness in 1454, Richard, third Duke of York and the father of King Henry IV and King Richard III, was made Protector of the Realm. England suffered civil war after the House of York challenged King Henry VI's right to be King of England. In 1470, King Henry VI was briefly restored to the English throne. In 1471, he was murdered in the Tower of London. A short time previously, his son, Edward, Prince of Wales, had been killed at the Battle of Tewkesbury in 1471; this was the final battle in the Wars of the Roses. The Yorkists decisively defeated the Lancastrians.

King Henry VI founded both Eton College and King's College, Cambridge.

# WARS OF THE ROSES

From 1455-1487, the Yorkists and the Lancastrians fought for power in England in the famous Wars of the Roses. The emblem of the York family was a white rose, and the emblem of the Lancaster family was a red rose. The Yorkists and the Lancastrians were descended from King Edward III.

# HOUSE OF YORK

**KING EDWARD IV: 1461-1483 (King Henry VI briefly returned to the throne in 1470-1471)**

Son of Richard, third Duke of York, he charged his brother George, Duke of Clarence, with treason and had him murdered in 1478. After dying suddenly, he left behind two sons aged 12 and 9, and five daughters.

His surviving two brothers in Shakespeare's play *Richard III* are these: 1) George, Duke of Clarence. Clarence is the second-oldest brother; and 2) Richard, Duke of Gloucester, and afterwards King Richard III. Gloucester is the youngest surviving brother.

William Caxton established the first printing press in Westminster during King Edward IV's reign.

## KING EDWARD V: 1483-1483

The eldest son of King Edward IV, he reigned for only two months, the shortest-lived monarch in English history. He was 13 years old. He and his younger brother, Richard, were murdered in the Tower of London. According to Shakespeare's play, their uncle, Richard, Duke of Gloucester, who became King Richard III, was responsible for their murders.

## KING RICHARD III: 1483-1485

Brother of King Edward IV, Richard, the Duke of Gloucester, declared the two Princes in the Tower of London — King Edward V and Richard, Duke of York — illegitimate and made himself King Richard III. In 1485, Henry Tudor, Earl of Richmond, a descendant of John of Gaunt, who was the father of King Henry IV, defeated King Richard III at the Battle of Bosworth Field in Leicestershire. King Richard III died in that battle.

King Richard III's father was Richard Plantagenet, Duke of York. His mother was Cecily Neville, Duchess of York.

King Richard III's death in the Battle of Bosworth Field is regarded as marking the end of the Middle Ages in England.

# A NOTE ON THE PLANTAGENETS

The first Plantagenet King was King Henry II (1154-1189). From 1154 until 1485, when King Richard III died, all English kings were Plantagenets. Both the Lancaster family and the York family were Plantagenets.

Geoffrey Plantagenet, Count of Anjou, was the founder of the House of Plantagenet. Geoffrey's son, Henry Curtmantle, became King Henry II of England, thereby founding the Plantagenet dynasty. Geoffrey wore a sprig of broom, a flowering shrub, as a badge; the Latin name for broom is *planta genista*, and from it the name "Plantagenet" arose.

The Plantagenet dynasty can be divided into three parts:

1154-1216: The Angevins. The Angevin Kings were Henry II, Richard I (Richard the Lionheart), and John 1.

1216-1399: The Plantagenets. These Kings ranged from King Henry III to King Richard II.

1399-1485: The Houses of Lancaster and of York. These Kings ranged from King Henry IV to King Richard III.

# BEGINNING OF THE TUDOR DYNASTY

**KING HENRY VII: 1485-1509**

When King Richard III fell at the Battle of Bosworth, Henry Tudor, Earl of Richmond, became King Henry VII. A Lancastrian, he married Elizabeth of York — young Elizabeth of York in *Richard III* — and united the two warring houses, York and Lancaster, thus ending the Wars of the Roses. One of his grandfathers was Sir Owen Tudor, who married Catherine of Valoise, widow of King Henry V.

**KING HENRY VIII: 1509-1547**

King Henry VIII had six wives. These are their fates: "Divorced, Beheaded, Died, Divorced, Beheaded, Survived." He divorced his first wife, Catherine of Aragon, so that he could marry Anne Boleyn. Because of this, England divorced itself from the Catholic Church, and King Henry VIII became the head of the Church of England. King Henry VIII had one son and two daughters, all of whom became rulers of England: Edward, daughter of Jane Seymour; Mary, daughter of Catherine of Aragon; and Elizabeth, daughter of Anne Boleyn.

**KING EDWARD VI: 1547-1553**

The son of Henry VIII and Jane Seymour, King Edward VI succeeded his father at the age of nine; a Council of Regency with his uncle, Duke of Somerset, styled Protector, ruled the government.

During King Edward VI's reign, Archbishop Thomas Cranmer wrote the 1549 Book of Common Prayer.

When King Edward VI died, Lady Jane Grey was proclaimed Queen, but she ruled for only nine days before being executed in 1554, aged 17. Mary, daughter of Catherine of Aragon, became Queen. She was Catholic, thus the attempt to make Lady Jane Grey, a Protestant, Queen.

**QUEEN MARY I (BLOODY MARY) 1553-1558**

Queen Mary I attempted to make England a Catholic nation again. Some Protestant bishops, including Archbishop Thomas Cranmer, were burnt at the stake, and other violence broke out, resulting in her being known as Bloody Mary.

## QUEEN ELIZABETH I: 1558-1603

The daughter of King Henry VIII and Anne Boleyn, Queen Elizabeth I was a popular Queen. In 1588, the English navy decisively defeated the Spanish Armada. England had many notable playwrights and poets, including William Shakespeare and Ben Jonson, during her reign. She never married and had no children.

# KING JAMES I OF ENGLAND: A MEMBER OF THE HOUSE OF STUART

## KING JAMES I OF ENGLAND AND VI OF SCOTLAND: 1603-1625

King James I of England was the son of Mary, Queen of Scots, and Lord Darnley. In 1605 Guy Fawkes and his Catholic co-conspirators were captured before they could blow up the Houses of Parliament; this was known as the Gunpowder Plot.

In 1611, during King James I's reign, the Authorized Version of the Bible (the King James Version) was completed.

Also during King James I's reign, in 1620 the Pilgrims sailed for America in their ship *The Mayflower*.

# A NOTE ON SHAKESPEARE

William Shakespeare lived under two monarchs: Queen Elizabeth I and King James I.

# APPENDIX B: ABOUT THE AUTHOR

It was a dark and stormy night. Suddenly a cry rang out, and on a hot summer night in 1954, Josephine, wife of Carl Bruce, gave birth to a boy — me. Unfortunately, this young married couple allowed Reuben Saturday, Josephine's brother, to name their first-born. Reuben, aka "The Joker," decided that Bruce was a nice name, so he decided to name me Bruce Bruce. I have gone by my middle name — David — ever since.

Being named Bruce David Bruce hasn't been all bad. Bank tellers remember me very quickly, so I don't often have to show an ID. It can be fun in charades, also. When I was a counselor as a teenager at Camp Echoing Hills in Warsaw, Ohio, a fellow counselor gave the signs for "sounds like" and "two words," then she pointed to a bruise on her leg twice. Bruise Bruise? Oh yeah, Bruce Bruce is the answer!

Uncle Reuben, by the way, gave me a haircut when I was in kindergarten. He cut my hair short and shaved a small bald spot on the back of my head. My mother wouldn't let me go to school until the bald spot grew out again.

Of all my brothers and sisters (six in all), I am the only transplant to Athens, Ohio. I was born in Newark, Ohio, and have lived all around Southeastern Ohio. However, I moved to Athens to go to Ohio University and have never left.

At Ohio U, I never could make up my mind whether to major in English or Philosophy, so I got a bachelor's degree with a double major in both areas, then I added a master's degree in English and a master's degree in Philosophy.

Currently, and for a long time to come (I eat fruits and veggies), I am spending my retirement writing books such as *Nadia Comaneci: Perfect 10*, *The Funniest People in Dance*, *Homer's* Iliad: *A Retelling in Prose*, and *William Shakespeare's* Othello: *A Retelling in Prose*.

By the way, my sister Brenda Kennedy writes romances such as *A New Beginning* and *Shattered Dreams*.

# APPENDIX C: SOME BOOKS BY DAVID BRUCE

**Retellings of a Classic Work of Literature**

Arden of Faversham: *A Retelling*

*Ben Jonson's* The Alchemist: *A Retelling*

*Ben Jonson's* The Arraignment, or Poetaster: *A Retelling*

*Ben Jonson's* Bartholomew Fair: *A Retelling*

*Ben Jonson's* The Case is Altered: *A Retelling*

*Ben Jonson's* Catiline's Conspiracy: *A Retelling*

*Ben Jonson's* The Devil is an Ass: *A Retelling*

*Ben Jonson's* Epicene: *A Retelling*

*Ben Jonson's* Every Man in His Humor: *A Retelling*

*Ben Jonson's* Every Man Out of His Humor: *A Retelling*

*Ben Jonson's* The Fountain of Self-Love, or Cynthia's Revels: *A Retelling*

*Ben Jonson's* The Magnetic Lady, or Humors Reconciled: *A Retelling*

*Ben Jonson's* The New Inn, or The Light Heart: *A Retelling*

*Ben Jonson's* Sejanus' Fall: *A Retelling*

*Ben Jonson's* The Staple of News: *A Retelling*

*Ben Jonson's* A Tale of a Tub: *A Retelling*

*Ben Jonson's* Volpone, or the Fox: *A Retelling*

*Christopher Marlowe's Complete Plays: Retellings*

*Christopher Marlowe's* Dido, Queen of Carthage: *A Retelling*

*Christopher Marlowe's* Doctor Faustus: *Retellings of the 1604 A-Text and of the 1616 B-Text*

*Christopher Marlowe's* Edward II: *A Retelling*

*Christopher Marlowe's* The Massacre at Paris: *A Retelling*

*Christopher Marlowe's* The Rich Jew of Malta: *A Retelling*

*Christopher Marlowe's* Tamburlaine, Parts 1 and 2: *Retellings*

*Dante's* Divine Comedy: *A Retelling in Prose*

*Dante's* Inferno: *A Retelling in Prose*

*Dante's* Purgatory: *A Retelling in Prose*

*Dante's* Paradise: *A Retelling in Prose*

The Famous Victories of Henry V: *A Retelling*

*From the* Iliad *to the* Odyssey: *A Retelling in Prose of Quintus of Smyrna's* Posthomerica

*George Chapman, Ben Jonson, and John Marston's* Eastward Ho! *A Retelling*

*George Peele's* The Arraignment of Paris: *A Retelling*

*George Peele's* The Battle of Alcazar: *A Retelling*

*George's Peele's* David and Bathsheba, and the Tragedy of Absalom: *A Retelling*

*George Peele's* Edward I: *A Retelling*

*George Peele's* The Old Wives' Tale: *A Retelling*

*William Shakespeare's 38 Plays: Retellings in Prose*
*William Shakespeare's 1 Henry IV, aka Henry IV, Part 1: A Retelling in Prose*
*William Shakespeare's 2 Henry IV, aka Henry IV, Part 2: A Retelling in Prose*
*William Shakespeare's 1 Henry VI, aka Henry VI, Part 1: A Retelling in Prose*
*William Shakespeare's 2 Henry VI, aka Henry VI, Part 2: A Retelling in Prose*
*William Shakespeare's 3 Henry VI, aka Henry VI, Part 3: A Retelling in Prose*
*William Shakespeare's All's Well that Ends Well: A Retelling in Prose*
*William Shakespeare's Antony and Cleopatra: A Retelling in Prose*
*William Shakespeare's As You Like It: A Retelling in Prose*
*William Shakespeare's The Comedy of Errors: A Retelling in Prose*
*William Shakespeare's Coriolanus: A Retelling in Prose*
*William Shakespeare's Cymbeline: A Retelling in Prose*
*William Shakespeare's Hamlet: A Retelling in Prose*
*William Shakespeare's Henry V: A Retelling in Prose*
*William Shakespeare's Henry VIII: A Retelling in Prose*
*William Shakespeare's Julius Caesar: A Retelling in Prose*
*William Shakespeare's King John: A Retelling in Prose*
*William Shakespeare's King Lear: A Retelling in Prose*
*William Shakespeare's Love's Labor's Lost: A Retelling in Prose*
*William Shakespeare's Macbeth: A Retelling in Prose*
*William Shakespeare's Measure for Measure: A Retelling in Prose*
*William Shakespeare's The Merchant of Venice: A Retelling in Prose*
*William Shakespeare's The Merry Wives of Windsor: A Retelling in Prose*
*William Shakespeare's A Midsummer Night's Dream: A Retelling in Prose*
*William Shakespeare's Much Ado About Nothing: A Retelling in Prose*
*William Shakespeare's Othello: A Retelling in Prose*
*William Shakespeare's Pericles, Prince of Tyre: A Retelling in Prose*
*William Shakespeare's Richard II: A Retelling in Prose*
*William Shakespeare's Richard III: A Retelling in Prose*
*William Shakespeare's Romeo and Juliet: A Retelling in Prose*
*William Shakespeare's The Taming of the Shrew: A Retelling in Prose*
*William Shakespeare's The Tempest: A Retelling in Prose*
*William Shakespeare's Timon of Athens: A Retelling in Prose*
*William Shakespeare's Titus Andronicus: A Retelling in Prose*
*William Shakespeare's Troilus and Cressida: A Retelling in Prose*
*William Shakespeare's Twelfth Night: A Retelling in Prose*
*William Shakespeare's The Two Gentlemen of Verona: A Retelling in Prose*
*William Shakespeare's The Two Noble Kinsmen: A Retelling in Prose*
*William Shakespeare's The Winter's Tale: A Retelling in Prose*